DEATH OF THE LAST VILLISTA

Also by Allana Martin

Death of a Myth Maker
Death of an Evangelista
Death of a Saint Maker
Death of a Healing Woman

DEATH OF THE LAST VILLISTA

Allana Martin

Thomas Dunne Books
St. Martin's Minotaur New York

THOMAS DUNNE BOOKS.
An imprint of St. Martin's Press.

www.minotaurbooks.com

Library of Congress Cataloging-in-Publication Data

Martin, Allana.
Death of the last villista : a Texana Jones mystery / Allana Martin.— 1st ed.
p. cm.
ISBN 0-312-26573-5
1. Jones, Texana (Fictitious character)—Fiction. 2. Villa, Pancho, 1878–1923—In motion pictures—Fiction. 3. Women detectives—Texas—Fiction. 4. Presidio County (Tex.)—Fiction. 5. Motion picture industry—Fiction. I. Title.

PS3563.A72319 D46 2001
813'.54—dc21

2001019256

First Edition: August 2001

10 9 8 7 6 5 4 3 2 1

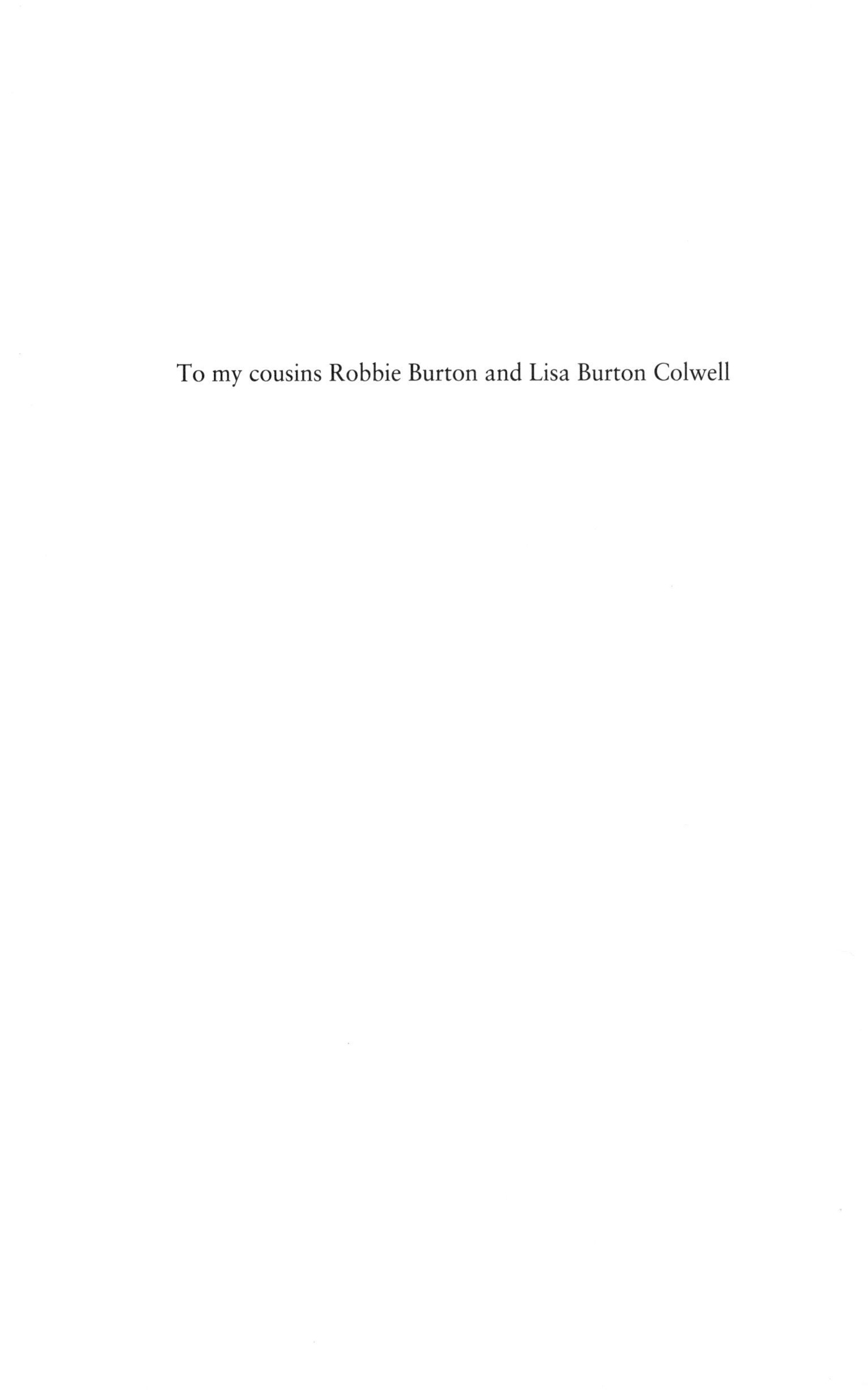

To my cousins Robbie Burton and Lisa Burton Colwell

Acknowledgments

Thanks are due to the following people for information used in the writing of this book: Joni L. McClain, M.D., Institute of Forensic Sciences, Dallas; child psychologist D. I. Little; Jamey Cantrell, operational director, Humane Society of North Texas; Lieutenant Daylon McCreless, fire and arson investigator, Austin Fire Department; John Wynn, Investigative Division, Texas State Fire Marshal's Office; and Christopher Hamilton with Advanced Communication Group, Inc., Arlington, for his videography expertise.

Special thanks go to Kevin Buchanan, D.V.M., and his staff at the Bowie Drive Animal Hospital and Pet Resort, Weatherford, Texas, not only for providing information about veterinary medicine used in this book, but for keeping the companion of our quiet hours, Hink E. the Cat, healthy into her twenty-first year.

Autentica Oracion al Espiritu de Pancho Villa
(Authentic Prayer to the Spirit of Pancho Villa)

Great General who triumphed over the powerful, I call for your spiritual protection that I may be spared from evil and find the courage and valor of Villa to face the difficulties of life. May I overthrow my enemies as you overthrew yours. Pancho Villa, pray for me.

—*from a prayer card commonly sold in marketplaces in northern Mexico*

PROLOGUE

An article from the June 6, 1961, Big Bend Sentinel, *the weekly newspaper published in Marfa, Texas.*

Polveños Welcome Hollywood

POLVO—The entire population of this tiny hamlet on the Rio Grande welcomed Hollywood stars Rosalinda Pray, Jeff Win, and Dane Anthony on Wednesday as they arrived to begin filming portions of the movie *Panchito,* about the 1917 raid on the Moore ranch by the forces of Pancho Villa. The movie is based on an account of the event in the best-selling book *The Centaur of the North* by author Calixto Sellis.

Locals will be familiar with the story of Ernestine Moore, kidnapped during one of the worst of the early twentieth-century border raids. At dawn on June 10, Mexican bandits hit the Moore ranch, and after a valiant fight by foreman Cal Teller, known ever after as "Tenacious" Teller, the invaders looted the ranch store and killed Mickey Kelly, the driver of the mail wagon, and his two passengers as they arrived during the shoot-out. The bandits escaped on horseback down one of the steep canyons, crossing back into Mexico and taking Mrs. Moore with them. The ranch foreman heard one of the bandits shout, "*Viva Villa!*" as the raiding party rode out. Mrs. Moore was later released unharmed after her husband arranged a ransom payment.

Members of the film crew and the newly arrived stars were entertained at a barbecue and dance held on the Darke ranch and hosted by Leigh and Bob Darke. Some of the film's outdoor scenes will be shot in the scenic canyons and among the high mountains of the ranch, one of the area's largest holdings, located ten miles above Polvo.

In April, only two short months after the director and his aides finished site selection for the film, work crews arrived and began re-creating a Mexican village of the early part of the century on land belonging to Justice and Sally Ricciotti, owners of the trading post below Polvo, where crew members are being housed in nearby trailers brought in by Garner Studio.

The stars and producer-director Jon French will stay in private homes belonging to prominent local ranchers Holmes and Estefina Wesleco, Carter Masters, Tom and Nan Putnam, and Jason and Pauline Marks. Garner Studio leased the entire Three Palms Inn in Presidio for four weeks, the projected filming time, for featured players, including actor Rudolf Montoya, who plays the part of one of Villa's trusted captains, known as the *Dorados* or "Golden Ones," and members of the technical staff. Visiting executives will stay at the Paisano Hotel in Marfa and be transported to the filming sites by private car.

Authenticity is important to director Jon French, who has hired a former follower of Villa, Jacinto Trejo, to act as consultant. Trejo joined Villa's forces as a boy of ten or eleven, fighting as a *revolucionario* in the *Division del Norté*.

Fifty-two Polveños have been hired as extras for the movie, and carpenters, *adoberos,* and laborers from both sides of the river have been employed to supplement the construction crew. Additionally, local ranchers are supplying horses and cattle to be used during the filming.

ONE

At 6:00 A.M., with an hour to go before sunrise, I turned on the light switch and flipped the CLOSED sign to OPEN without so much as a glance through the glass half of the double doors, which explains why I didn't see the white envelope lying on the porch.

Cold hugged the corners of the trading post and layered the floor like a blanket as the warmth from the propane heaters at either end of the three-thousand-square-foot space rose toward the ceiling rafters. I shivered slightly in my thick sweater as I brewed a pot of coffee for the four ranchers who met here every Tuesday. In addition to coffee, I sell ranch and veterinary supplies, clothes, groceries, and gasoline at the trading post, which sits on a rise facing the black asphalt ribbon of Ranch Road 170. Two miles west, at the very end of the road, is Polvo, a tiny community of 125 people. From there, empty miles stretch all the way to El Paso.

The members of the Tuesday coffee group drive long miles

from various directions to get together. Distance and time dominate life here in the borderland, *la frontera.* We have three county roads and two state highways. The rest of our nearly four thousand square miles is privately owned ranch land measured in sections rather than acres.

My name is Texana Jones. I'm a *fronterizo* born and raised on a section of land bought in 1888 by my paternal great-grandfather, Franco Ricciotti, who left Italy with no regrets, worked as a stonemason in Texas and Chihuahua, and selected the best of both worlds by settling on the Rio Grande, the boundary of both. To build the trading post that would also be his home, he hired laborers from the closest village across the river. They cut cottonwood trees along the greenbelt to frame the building. Great-grandfather roofed it in sheet tin, driving in the square-headed nails himself, and opened for business the same year. His customers came from both sides of the river to barter lechuguilla fiber ropes, goat hides, and furs brought in by mules for piece goods and staples of salt, lard, flour, and beans. Twice a month my great-grandfather rode his mule into Presidio to court the teacher who became his wife. After their marriage, they lived in the same quarters in which I grew up and where I have lived for the past eighteen years with my husband Clay, a veterinarian who moved here as an adult but loves the place almost as much as I do. We don't make much of a living by most people's standards, having downscaled our lifestyle long before it was trendy, but we do live "much of a life," as my friend Pete Rosales likes to say.

When the coffeemaker finished the brewing cycle, I poured a cup for myself and took my seat on the stool behind the counter. I was barely halfway through the cup when the first of the ranchers arrived. Hugh Wesleco brought a puff of cold air in with him. An exceptionally tall man, he wore a stained cowboy hat, quilted vest, plaid flannel shirt and jeans, and heavy boots that thudded against the floorboards as he came down the center aisle waving an envelope in the air.

"You got a secret admirer, Texana? Somebody's left you a love note under a rock on the porch out there."

He dropped a plain white envelope, my name printed on it in black felt tip pen, on the counter in front of me and went to pour himself a cup of coffee.

As Hugh pulled out a chair at the table in front of the heater, two more ranchers ambled in—Ed Wyler, paunchy and balding, and Hap Boyer, small and brown like an aged elf, with a voice like a sonic boom. They wished me good-morning, hung up their hats, and joined Hugh.

The envelope felt thin and empty. I tore it open at one end and extracted a folded sheet of white typing paper. It took me a mere second to read the one sentence, printed like my name:

Keep the movie people away
or what happens will be on you

"Pondering something serious?"

I looked up to find Hugh standing directly in front of the counter, his eyes on the sheet of paper, a speculative look on his face. Being a community of few, we are incorrigibly nosy about everyone else's business.

"Just lack of caffeine getting to me," I said, pushing the paper away from me and farther from Hugh's prying eyes. "I'm only halfway through my first cup."

Hugh pulled out a billfold so old the leather had cracked into hundreds of fine lines across the surface, extracted a fifty, and handed it over to me. I gave him his usual carton of Lucky Strike cigarettes and counted out his change. He put away his money, fished a matchbook out of his pocket, and was lighting up by the time he got back to the table.

Drawing the paper back to me, I read the terse sentence again, folded the paper, and tucked it under the cash drawer, then looked up to smile at Johnny Salvo as he joined the others.

Over the next hour the ranchers drank cup after cup of coffee while they complained about the weather, bemoaned cattle prices, speculated on the dropping water table, fumed about the increase in low-level flyovers by the German air force pilots training out of New Mexico, and discussed the failed project to extend our river road by forty miles.

When the third pot of coffee was empty, they came to the register to pay.

"Don't forget," I reminded them as I rang up the sale, "that I'll be closed all next week."

"We know," Hap said, slapping Hugh on the back lightly. "Old Hugh here is gonna be famous after they put his ugly mug on the TV. He's gonna have the ladies writing to propose." Hap nudged his friend Johnny Salvo. "Too bad you and me weren't in the movie like Texana and Hugh so we could be on TV, too."

"I'm not going to be on television," Hugh said flatly.

"A might shy about talking in front of a camera, eh?" Hap grinned broadly, expecting a comeback. Hugh ignored him.

"Everybody else'll talk enough to make up for it," Johnny said. "I bet Texana's been practicing in front of the mirror."

I was used to the good-natured kidding. I'd been hearing it for weeks from most of my customers. An independent video producer was going to make a PBS special celebrating the fortieth anniversary of the Hollywood movie *Panchito,* which in 1961 had been the biggest event to hit our area since the border bandit raids. Our moment of fame had been more fleeting then usual. The movie had died early at the box office. The single justification for the PBS special was the recent resurrection of Dane Anthony's career. Out of the public eye for decades, the actor who played Pancho Villa had suddenly surfaced on television, playing a grandfather on a hit half-hour comedy called *Leo's Family,* now in its third year.

This according to Scott Regan, the independent video producer in charge of the project. He had arrived at the trading post in early summer, asking about the film's original sites and searching out locals who had participated in it. Since then he had made two more trips to conduct preliminary interviews.

Next Monday he and his crew would arrive and take over the trading post for their video project.

"It's good luck for you," Hap said to me, "that your dad let 'em use his land for the movie. Make 'em pay up front, I say, for using it again."

"Are they staying here?" Johnny asked.

"They're bringing RVs."

"Perfect guests," Hap said cheerfully. "Bringing their own beds. Can't beat that."

I smiled, but only weakly. I wasn't sure it was worth giving up my privacy and the normal quiet of our days, but I had felt obligated to the community to cooperate. The least economic boost is a boon to us. Especially to me. Scott Regan's production company had offered compensation for the use of the trading post and access to the portions of my land where the original moviemakers had constructed a group of adobes to resemble a tiny Mexican village of the early 1900s. I was getting one thousand dollars up front, and another five hundred when the taping, expected to take a week to ten days, was completed. This in addition to the fifteen-dollars-per-day hookup fee for each of the video crew's RVs. The money wasn't half as much as my parents had been paid in '61 by the movie producers, but a welcome increase in my income nonetheless.

"I heard two of the movie actors are coming back," Hap said. "Is that right?"

"That's right," I told him. "The two stars, Dane Anthony and Rosalinda Pray."

"Never heard of either one of them," Johnny said. "And me and the wife, we got a wall of movie videos in the living room."

"The Anthony fellow made a bunch of spaghetti westerns in the late sixties," Ed said. "I don't know what happened to the woman."

"I'd just gone to work for the Border Patrol back when they were making the movie," Hap said. "I don't recall much about it except for the murder. I helped to collect the body. Man named Trejo."

"Who was he?" Johnny said.

"Some *villista* working with the movie people," Hap said. "That was my first dead body. I'll never forget it. Some kids playing in the river found him on No Man's Land. Me and this other agent went out there. Thought he was a floater that washed up until we turned him over and saw the side of his head had been bashed in."

No Man's Land is a small island in the middle of the river with a fine stand of marijuana growing on it. It is claimed as territory by neither Mexico nor the United States.

"When no family showed up," Hap added, "there was a flap over who would pay for burying him, Mexico or us. Finally, the movie people paid for taking the body back to Mexico."

That pushed the conversation toward the inequities of border law, including a new one by Mexico that charges everyone entering fifteen dollars. Moving back and forth as often as we do, we *fronterizos* grumble at the charge. We tend to think of both sides of the border as our country and the idea of the river as a boundary as something made up in *Chilangolandia* or *Washingtolandia*, our derisive terms for Mexico City and Washington.

Finally, the ranchers took the conversation with them out the door. The remainder of the morning passed quietly and unremarkably. Over the course of four hours I sold a pair of welding gloves, a three-quarter-inch fuel nozzle, and a tow chain. Three customers paid late fees on the returns of movie rentals, all of them copies of *Panchito* I had ordered; three others were on the rental waiting list. There had been enough interest in the movie that I hadn't been able to watch it myself. Even Hugh, who had refused to participate in the anniversary video, had rented a copy. We were both nine when we had been selected as extras in the film. It had been exciting, though I had forgotten most of the details of those days.

At noon I retired to our private quarters at the back of the trading post, leaving the front door unlocked so anyone needing something could come through and find me. Except for new plumbing and wiring for electricity, the narrow rooms that make up our living space are still much as my great-grandfather built them.

Our pet bobcat sprawled on the back of the couch, legs dangling. Hearing my footsteps, her whiskers twitched, her round eyes opened, and she gave a throaty *me-ooph*. I walked past her into the galley kitchen. She leaped down and padded after me to nip my ankle, a reminder that her food bowl was empty.

Raised from a kitten by another family, she is named Phobe because everyone is afraid of her, though she is as gentle as a pussycat. She has the run of the place, which explains why the furniture has a slightly chewed look.

I filled up her pan with some chopped chunks of the mix of horse meat, vitamins, and minerals that Clay orders through a wholesaler that supplies zoos.

While Phobe smacked loudly, I made roast chicken sandwiches on toasted bread and tossed together a salad of corn, black beans, onions, and canned salsa.

As I was preparing the iced tea, I heard a pickup door slam out back. Clay's clinic is a trailer behind the trading post. To one side are pens and a squeeze shoot for doctoring large animals. On the other side is a short row of cement-block kennels. Clay's veterinary practice is mostly with cattle and horses. Since the ranch hands do much of the livestock doctoring, vet supplies are one of my biggest selling items. Clay is called out primarily for emergencies, in cases where surgery may be needed, for diagnostic advice, and for vaccinations required by law.

"What's for lunch?" Clay said as he came in.

Clay is six-foot-one, straight and slim, with gray hair thinning a little on top, though I doubt that he will ever be bald. His features are strong: hooded green eyes, a prominent nose, and firm mouth. He jokes and laughs a lot despite the fact that he is a worrier who takes things to heart.

"How's the dog?" I asked.

"If he makes it through the next three days, he'll be okay," Clay said, eying the food as I put things on the table. "I left the owner with vitamin K capsules to counteract the rat poison and a strong recommendation to get a cat."

After we finished the meal, Clay settled on the couch. Phobe pounced on him, bumping his chin with her head in a typical bobcat greeting. She stretched luxuriously as he ruffled her tawny coat. I left them to go to the front and get the note.

"What do you make of this?" I said, handing Clay the folded sheet of paper and telling him how it had arrived.

His eyes swept it, then he looked up at me. "How much does this worry you?"

"I don't know. It doesn't read as a specific threat against me. It's like the writer wants to stop the video being made."

Clay glanced at the sentence again. "It doesn't say anything about the video. It says 'the movie people.' Maybe the writer means those two actors, Pray and Anthony."

"Or the writer doesn't know the difference between a video and a film. I suppose I should tell Scott," I said.

Clay stretched an arm along the back of the couch and stroked Phobe's ears with his other hand. "Just remember," he said emphatically, "threats are like rattlesnakes. Some warn you and never strike. But some do. Best wear your boots, just in case."

TWO

At midday Monday, two motor homes, both bigger than most of the adobes in Polvo and one towing a blue Range Rover, pulled into the RV lot. They were followed closely by a red Suburban towing a silver trailer. Scott Regan and his crew had arrived.

Clay and I went out to the porch to welcome them. The still November day had warmed from an overnight low of twenty-eight to nearly ninety. By late afternoon it would be above that mark. Our extended summer heat pushes late into fall along the river.

Scott Regan, a dark, bespectacled young man in his mid-twenties, dressed in wheat-colored shirt, cuffed chinos, and lace-up boots, stepped out of one of the motor homes and extended a hand to a slim young woman behind him. She touched a hand to her cropped pink hair and stared at her surroundings as if in disbelief. In turn, I looked at her in some awe noting the number of silver rings that pierced her ears, more than I have in my jewelry box. But it was the nose ring that made me wince with empathetic pain. The last thing I'd seen with a nose ring was a black bull, and he hadn't appreciated the decoration. Two more men looking about Scott's age emerged from the second motor home. A fourth, older-looking man stepped from the Suburban and followed the others up the front steps of the trading post.

Smiling hugely, Scott shook our hands and introduced his crew.

"This is Jeremy Win. His dad was Jeff Win, Captain Ortega in *Panchito.*"

I smiled at the man who had been driving the Suburban. He kept his hands in his pockets and gave a curt nod, turning his head to stare at the river, and showing me the bald spot that shone like a tonsure in his brown hair.

"Jere is our still photographer. Have I told you we're doing a book in conjunction with the video? Jere has a complete darkroom in that trailer of his," Scott said. "And this is my assistant, Jenna Hart."

The colorful young woman shifted her attention from the river to us. "It took so long to get here," she said, "I thought Scott must be playing a joke."

"Our videographers, Ben Grant and Chris Hall."

Ben was short, solemn-looking, and tending to overweight. Chris was nearly as tall as Clay, with the face of a twelve-year-old. Both wore knit shirts and jeans, which on Ben looked comfortable and on Chris looked stylish.

We invited them in, going straight to our quarters. For lunch I'd made *guiso,* a fragrant pork stew, and guacamole salad. As we settled around the table, Jenna announced, "I'm vegan."

"She doesn't eat meat," Scott explained.

"I assumed it wasn't an astrological sign," I said, passing Jenna the salad. As we ate Scott explained his schedule to Clay and me.

"We'll be taping interviews with thirty-eight of your local

people. Starting at eight, we'll do three each morning, and in the afternoons, three, maybe four if time allows. I've roughed out a schedule of names and times. There'll be some evening tapings to accommodate those who work in Presidio."

After lunch, Scott gave us a tour of the two motor homes. The one he shared with Jenna was spacious and had all the comforts, including a kitchen that I coveted, but it was the second one that impressed me with the seriousness of their project. What would have been a living room had been refitted as office space filled with all the electronic equipment needed for editing the videocassettes.

After the tour, Clay left for his office to examine a puppy brought in by a mother and three small children. The rest of us went to work removing everything from about a third of my display tables and freestanding shelves and stacking them on top of other merchandise. Chris seemed fascinated by my inventory of veterinary supplies housed in an antique wooden cabinet in the middle of the room. I explained that ranch hands took care of their own animals by and large, which meant that things like wound spray, iodine solution, vaccines and antibiotics, hypodermic needles, and electrolyte products for oral rehydration were some of my best-selling items. He spent so much time reading labels on some of the products that Scott kidded him about "going to veterinary school" after the video was done. Chris grinned good-naturedly and went back to work. As each table was emptied, Scott, Chris, and Ben moved it outside and covered it in plastic sheeting weighted down by rocks and boards. The plastic was to protect the wood from the sun. Our rainfall is scant, seven inches a year, and we'd had less than that for the past five, so damp was my least concern.

This made room for the crew to set up recording equipment and the large video camera, which Ben called a "Betacam," and to create what Scott referred to as a stage area. Jeremy photographed us as we worked.

It was three before we finished and retired to the porch for iced tea. The crew were relaxed and jovial. I felt like a real spoiler as I took the warning note from my pocket.

"Someone left this for me last week," I said, handing it to Scott. "I thought I'd better show it to you."

He shoved his glasses up on his nose and bent his head over it, a movement that caused both wings of his dark hair to fall forward like blinders on a racehorse. Jenna, seated next to him, leaned across his arm to read.

"What is it?" Chris asked, and Scott read it aloud. I had to admit that, without the heavy black letters in front of me, it sounded less serious, more like something a kid might have written. Scott handed it back to me with a reassuring smile.

"I wouldn't give it another thought. Maybe someone wanted to worry you a bit. Take some of the fun out of the week. Probably a meaningless prank. Or a bad joke. It's pretty vague, isn't it," he said, half-grinning.

At his words, Chris smiled at me, as if backing up Scott's grin. Jenna relaxed instantly. If Scott says it, it must be so was apparently her credo. Only Ben appeared solemn, but then, so far that had been his only expression. Jeremy remained quiet, sitting apart as if aloof from his younger companions.

"It's the generality I find a little scary. Like the writer isn't sure what he's capable of."

"I'm sure it's nothing," Scott said dismissively.

I tucked the note back into my pocket. Scott got to his feet. "We'd better get back to work. We'll see you at the party tonight."

"Thanks again for lunch," Jenna said as the crew took off for their RVs. I sat on the porch for a few more minutes, watching Jeremy, who'd paused to photograph the river. When he turned the camera toward the trading post, I went in to wash the lunch dishes.

At four-thirty Scott and his crew unhitched the Rover, loaded another camera, tripod, and recorder, and left for Presidio to set up for the party Scott had arranged to welcome Rosalinda Pray and Dane Anthony.

An hour later a steady line of vehicles, each packed tightly with people, began passing the trading post, headed toward Presidio. Polvo didn't want to be late to the party. Clay had come in to shower. We changed into our party clothes. He wore a moss green turtleneck sweater, charcoal gray pants, and a suede blazer in a warm gray, a gift from his sister Fran. I wore a brightly woven tunic from Oaxaca over a long red skirt. By six we had locked up and were on our way.

THREE

Tia's Cafe looked like a supermarket on triple coupon day. Standing room only.

Clay and I bypassed the receiving line, where the efficient and amiable young producer and his assistant stood almost flattened against a shocking-pink wall by the crush of their guests.

As we inched through the crowd, past tables already decorated with paper flowers and loaded with plates of appetizers, I saw everyone I knew from Polvo except the children, leaving me to wonder who had been left to baby-sit. A hospitality bar had been set up, and the single bartender had as much as he could do to keep up with the orders. Conversation flowed as freely as the liquor and competed in volume with a *norteño conjuntos* group. The stand-up bass, guitarist, and accordianist, hired to wander through the crowd but finding themselves trapped by it, played enthusiastically in one corner. From a platform to one side, Ben captured it all on videotape.

Chris saw us and made his way to our side. "Great place,

but a little tight on space," he said. "I was checking out the head table. There doesn't seem to be a microphone. Jenna seems to think there should be."

"Don't worry," Clay said. "We'll be able to hear."

From the head table, Scott requested, in an unamplified voice, that everyone take their seats.

"Too late to worry about a mike," Chris said, and excused himself to go and help Ben.

Those closest to the head table did as Scott asked. The rest of the crowd shifted their attention away from conversations to what was going on at the head table. Slowly, chairs scraped against the linoleum floor until everyone was seated.

I found myself next to Eva Ybarra, at eighty-two very much the matriarch of Polvo. Across from us sat white-haired Tom Putnam, his son, and the son's new and much younger third wife, who was already looking bored.

"Quite a turnout," Gwen Masters said in her smoker's voice as she hobbled up and squeezed in on Clay's other side.

"How's the new knee, Gwen?" Tom asked.

"Hurts like a mule kick," she said, twisting to hook her cane over the back of her chair.

"It's wonderful," Eva said, "how doctors can replace knee and hip joints nowadays."

"The physical therapy is worse than the surgery," Gwen said, frowning at the "No Smoking Please" sign on the table, her fingers pulling back from a bulging pocket.

Gwen was a hands-on rancher, as weathered as any *vaquero*. Completely comfortable with herself, she had stayed with her normal attire of jacket, shirt, and slacks, though I noticed her boots had been polished.

Scott tapped a spoon against a glass to get our attention once more. He made a brief welcoming speech, introducing his associates and explaining that the finished video would be shown on public television near the anniversary date of the long-ago premiere of *Panchito*.

"As you may know," he said, "the charismatic Rudolf

Montoya died in a car accident only days before the film opened . . ."

"Lucky man," said a wheezing voice behind us.

". . . Director Jon French died in nineteen-eighty-nine. Actor Jeff Win only recently passed away, but fortunately we have the two stars of the movie here in person. Please welcome Rosalinda Pray and Dane Anthony."

The *conjuntos* struck up something that sounded like bullring music, and the room throbbed with applause as a skinny woman in an emerald green suit that fitted like a body-wrap appeared from the manager's office. She clutched a small brown-and-white dog to her chest. Beside her was a white-haired man in a wheelchair.

"She looks just the same," Eva said.

A huge man in an ill-fitting gray suit stepped forward to push the wheelchair to the table. Rosalinda Pray walked alongside, her head tilted, her chin tucked in modestly, an expression of surprised gratitude on her face as she acknowledged the crowd. The dog squirmed slightly in her arms. As his wheelchair was propelled forward, Dane Anthony smiled broadly and waved with both hands. The blue suit he wore set off his tanned skin.

Dane Anthony's attendant eased the wheelchair into position next to Scott. Rosalinda Pray thrust the dog into Scott's hands, turned blue eyes on her old acquaintance, and bent to kiss him on the cheek, then applauded him with the rest of the crowd. Scott stepped back, holding the dog away from him, then passed it to a waiter behind him. He grabbed a napkin and rubbed at his slacks where a dark stain had spread. The dog had peed on him.

Oblivious to this minor disaster, Rosalinda Pray stepped forward, gave the room a sweeping glance, and raised her arms as if to embrace us all. "I can't tell you how glad I am to be here. I have so many wonderful memories of this place," she said, her soft voice not carrying much beyond the third row of tables.

Scott pulled out a chair for her, and she sat down, looking around, then beckoned to the waiter, who looked relieved to give up the dog to its owner.

At our table Eva leaned across to Gwen. "What was it she said about us in that newspaper interview back when the movie was being made?"

"Said we were 'charmingly parochial,' " Gwen answered. "Made us sound like a bunch of yahoos."

There was a moment of respectful silence as Dane Anthony's aide helped the actor to his feet. His body might have betrayed him, but his magnificent voice had not. The actor delivered a gracious speech saying how elated he was to be back among the friends who had so helped in the making of what he considered the most important movie of his career.

As the actor continued to speak, cameras flashed as both locals and the single reporter representing the county weekly newspaper captured the moment.

The applause swelled again as he sat down. The wait staff began serving dinner, and again the wheezy voice spoke: "The only interesting thing about *Panchito* was the murder."

FOUR

I glanced around as if looking for the waiter and found the source of the voice, a large man at the next table. He was seated with his back to me. The portable oxygen tank next to his chair explained the breathless voice. I turned to ask Eva if she knew him, but she was talking with Jose Reyes, seated on her other side.

Gwen tossed back the last of her gin and tonic. "During the filming you'd have thought Dane Anthony had been born here. He was that friendly and natural. Knew all our first names and told us to call him by his. Her, now, she was just the opposite. Never came out of that trailer without her nose in the air."

"I wonder what put Anthony in that chair?" Tom asked.

"Polio," I said. "Scott told me that Dane had it as a child, in the days before the vaccine. It was a mild case with no apparent effects in his youth, but it seems that some of the symptoms come back with age."

"How tragic," Tom Putnam's new daughter-in-law said.

I leaned away from the table as the waitress slipped a plate of *tamales con chorizo* in front of me.

"I had such a crush on him," Gwen said. "I guess all us girls did. Including Rosalinda Pray. She hugged all over him. It didn't surprise me when the newspapers came out with a story right before the movie premiere about them having a love affair during the filming. She and Dane were getting their pictures in all the papers."

"She married someone else," Eva said.

Gwen gave a contemptuous snort. "There's no accounting for taste."

"You ladies are too hard on Miss Rosalinda," Jose Reyes said, looking into the distance as if seeing a vision. "She was a feast for the eyes."

"You men," Eva retorted, "couldn't see past those twenty-three-year-old blue eyes of hers."

Jose chuckled and said, "It wasn't only her eyes."

"Life was downright dull around here after the movie folks left," Gwen said. "Rudolf Montoya stayed at the ranch, you know. Dad took him out hunting for a cougar that had been getting our calves. Montoya got the cat through the heart with his first shot. Said he did skeet shooting back in California. Dad thought enough of him to send flowers to the funeral."

"I went to Señor Trejo's funeral in Cuchillo Parado," Tom said. "He was only in his fifties. Too young to die."

"That's right," Gwen said. "He and the director, Jon French, stayed at your place, didn't they?"

"They used to stay up late talking about Villa and the revolution," Tom said. "Trejo claimed he lived through the fighting because he had a good luck charm that protected him from the devil and disaster."

"Did he lose it or did it just stop working for him?" Gwen said.

"I was stunned when he was killed. I assumed somebody thought he carried a lot of money because of his association with the movie," Tom said. "But his money and identification hadn't been taken."

"Who killed him?" Clay asked.

Tom shook his head. "They never found out."

"If it wasn't robbery, it must have been something to do with drugs," I said.

"Why do you say that?" Tom's daughter-in-law asked.

"Along the border most of the crime and two-thirds of the prosperity involves drugs," I said.

"Do you remember Señor Trejo, Texana?" Eva asked.

"Vaguely, but I don't recall much about the murder."

"No wonder," Gwen said. "There were lots of killings along the river in those days. Ojinaga was full up with drug lords shooting anyone who looked at them sideways. I bet poor Señor Trejo saw something he shouldn't have."

"Or was involved in something he shouldn't have been. That's what the authorities suspected," Tom said. "I was saddened. I genuinely liked the man. But one never knows. The lure of drug money. . . . Before the murder, Garner Studio's publicity people couldn't get enough of Trejo. In their press releases they dubbed him *The Last Villista.* Said he must be the last living Villa follower because he had joined the revolutionaries when he was only ten or eleven. The newspaper and TV reporters picked up on that and ran with it. Which irritated Trejo to no end. He tried explaining to French that there were a lot of young boys among the revolutionaries, so he could hardly be the only one still living. French just smiled and said he never complained about good press." Tom shook his head. "But after the gossip started that Trejo might have been killed because he was smuggling drugs in someone else's territory, the studio's public relations flacks stifled the publicity and tried to erase him from the public's mind. French warned the actors and crew not to give interviews. He closed the last days of filming to the media. The studio even dropped Trejo's name from the film's credits as if he'd never been a part of it all."

We sat quietly for a moment, then Gwen broke the silence.

"I shouldn't have another G&T," she said, motioning to a waiter, "but I'm going to. I never had one until the movie people served them at the farewell party."

We finished the meal to a steady flow of happier reminiscences about the movie days.

As dessert was served Scott got to his feet and called for our attention again. "The evening is almost over. I speak not only for myself but also my video crew when I say that we look forward to working with you all." He raised his glass. "Here's to all those who helped make *Panchito.*"

Dane Anthony offered a second toast. "To the video project, and to the memories of Pancho Villa and my dear friends Rudolf Montoya and Jeff Win."

That was the last toast. As soon as dessert was finished the staff began clearing the tables, but the dining room wasn't emptying. Too many people were trying to speak with Rosalinda Pray and Dane Anthony.

Clay was talking cattle prices with Tom. I got up to stretch my legs and find the rest room. As I worked my way through the crowd I saw the wheezing man again, this time from the front. His skin hung in folds, like a suit one size too large. As he talked his jowls moved loosely. The reporter from the local newspaper was listening intently, shaking his head now and then as if in disbelief, sometimes nodding in agreement.

"*Variety* headlined it 'Texas Laughito' and 'Dane's Doom,' " the wheezy voice was saying as I passed by. "It ruined his career and sank hers before it was afloat."

I got to within ten feet of the rest-room door. That was where the line started. I gave it five minutes, during which we moved about one inch, before deciding I could wait. I found Clay and gave him the signal it was time to leave.

Once we were past the narrow band of lights that made up Presidio, the night settled in all around us except for the high beams of the headlights cutting into the darkness ahead. The drive home was uneventful. Because of the frequent dips, our road had to be traveled so slowly that there was no danger of hitting a varmint crossing the pavement to reach the river, though on this night the only living thing we saw was an owl gliding on open wings, hunting for foraging mice.

I told Clay about Scott's reaction to the warning note.

"If he's not worried, then why should we be?"

But I was, if not worried, at least anxious. As we neared home my heart beat a little faster. As the headlights hit the parking lot and the front porch, showing everything in its place, peaceful and normal, I relaxed with a sigh that Clay picked up on.

"Let's check out the RVs," he said, turning the pickup so the lights hit the motor homes and Jeremy Win's silver trailer.

"Everything looks okay to me," Clay said. I agreed.

We drove to the back of the trading post, parked, and got out. A coyote miles away on the other side of the river yipped in communion with the night. Suddenly he stopped, and the silence rushed in.

We went in, turned on the lights, and greeted a restless Phobe. Half an hour later I came out of the bathroom saying what a pleasant evening it had been. Clay didn't hear me. He lay on his side, asleep. Phobe was curled on top of the duvet at the foot of the bed. I slipped under the covers, put my back against Clay's, and felt for his warm feet with my cold ones.

Later the rushing sound of more traffic than normally passed by in a week woke me. Polvo was returning home from the party. It was nearly one-thirty when the slamming of car doors woke me a second time and I heard muted laughter and the voices of Scott and his crew.

FIVE

After breakfast, Clay announced that he was taking Phobe to stay with my father until the videotaping was finished.

"There'll be too many people going in and out," he said, lifting the bobcat into her carrier with a hand under her belly. "She might slip out and get lost."

I stacked the dishes in the sink, then went to the bedroom and searched among the boxes on the top shelf of the closet for something I had put away long ago. After my mother's sudden death from a heart attack when I was twenty-one, my father had closeted himself away from everyone and everything, leaving it to me to remove her clothes and pack away her personal possessions. I had kept only two boxes. They had been in the closet ever since. Not even when Scott Regan's first visit had resurrected my childhood memories of *Panchito* had I thought of them. Until last night. I lifted down the box marked "Photo Albums," put it on the bed, and removed the lid. Inside were three albums, each neatly labeled in my mother's rounded handwriting. The one I wanted was on top.

I carried the red leather album back to the living area, plumped up the pillows on the couch, put my feet up on the scarred coffee table, and turned the pages, looking at the photographs my mother had taken. Somewhere I still had her camera, a thirty-five-millimeter Canon.

The photographs ran sequentially, beginning with the construction of the mock adobe village on our land. I remembered watching with my mother as the workers unloaded the mud and straw bricks made in Mexico and brought across the river by pack mule to the site.

There were many candid shots taken during the filming, photographs of actors, film crew, and extras at work, relaxing between takes, at catered meals taken outside under tents, patiently posing with various Polveños. One showed Dane Anthony made up as Pancho Villa in mustache, sombrero, khaki uniform, crossed cartridge belts, boots, and spurs, astride a great black horse.

I smiled at the photo of me with my best friend, Maria Ortega, our hair parted in the middle and braided. We watched a makeup artist fitting a wig on Dane Anthony while Hugh Wesleco, already tall for his age, stood holding the actor's sombrero and looking immensely proud.

I turned the page. In the eight-by-ten enlargement, I sat in the saddle atop a white horse, smiling straight into the camera with that complete lack of self-consciousness that belongs uniquely to childhood.

On the opposite page was a group photo. Rosalinda Pray, in halter top, slacks, and sandals, and Dane Anthony, in sweatshirt, jeans, and sandals had posed with a compact, clean-shaven man with dark eyes that looked as intelligent as his smile was compelling. He might have been any age from thirty to fifty.

"Texana?" Ben stood at the doorway between the front and

our quarters. I set the album open on the coffee table and invited him in. He glanced down at the photograph.

"Is that Rudolf Montoya with Dane and Ms. Pray?"

"It's the *villista.* Jacinto Trejo."

Ben bent closer over the album. "That's you on the horse, isn't it?"

"Yes."

"These aren't bad. Who took them?"

"My mother. There are others. Look, if you like," I said.

He sat down beside me and turned slowly through the whole album. "This one of Dane Anthony," he said, turning back to that page. "Scott might be interested in it for the companion book. And some of the ones of Rosalinda Pray." What might have been a grin lit his serious face as he added drily, "She's invested a bit in the video so she gets equal time, so to speak. I don't suppose you have the negatives?"

"They might be in another box. I can look."

"Even without them, or if they've deteriorated, Jere could make copies of these. I think you should leave this out for Scott to look over." He put the album back on the table.

"I'll leave it right there," I said. "Now, what did you come to tell me?"

"To ask, actually. May we use one of your armchairs for the tapings?"

I helped Ben carry the chair to the front. In the open space where the shelves had been, a large video camera on a tripod faced the wall of shelves where I kept equine supplies: blankets, bridles, brushes, combs, shampoos, medicines, and feed. We placed the armchair there. The scene resembled a photographer's studio, though the lighting was much brighter. There were four adjustable lamps, one directed at the chair, one on either side, and one for backlighting. Thick extension cords ran everywhere. I left the crew to their work and went to wash the dishes.

I was drying my hands when Jenna came to get me for the

group photograph that Scott had arranged for the Polveños who'd been extras in *Panchito*. I put on a corduroy jacket over my white shirt and jeans, ran a comb through my hair, and joined the gathering on the porch. We had an audience of family and friends wandering the parking lot. Fortunately, the day was warm and nearly windless, making the atmosphere festive.

Jeremy Win lined us up on the steps in order of height, so I ended up on the back row.

The camera went to his eye, then he lowered it, saying irritably, "Will *somebody* remove the goat, please."

"Why don't you leave him for atmosphere," Jose Reyes said. "There were plenty of goats in *Panchito*. Probably this one's a relative."

A twelve-year-old boy, grinning sheepishly, ran out from the crowd of observers. His mother, Sixta Ramos, standing one step below me, yelled, "Jimmy Ramos! You cut school again!"

The boy quickly untied the rope that tethered the goat to the porch rail and led the animal away.

The photographer waited until the two had rejoined the spectators, then said, "Big smiles, please," and thirty-eight faces, mine included, froze as the automatic lens whirled through several shots and Chris simultaneously videotaped the moment.

"Thanks, folks," Scott said when the photographer signaled that he was done. "We'll have a print made for each of you. Texana's agreed to have you pick them up here. They'll be ready in about two weeks. Now, listen up. The individual interviews will be taped as posted on the bulletin board by the front doors. Jenna is handing out copies of the schedule so you won't forget to be here when we need you. Please don't leave if you're being taped this morning." He consulted his clipboard. "That's three people we need to remain. Jose Reyes, Eva Ybarra, and Gwen Masters. Thanks to all of you for coming out this morning."

Some of the crowd moved toward their vehicles, but most

remained, talking with one another and watching the various members of the crew as avidly as if they were movie stars.

An excited squeal from Jimmy Ramos caught everyone's attention. The boy stood by the road, staring with all his might at the approach of a huge motor home, towing a Nissan Pathfinder. Jeremy Win snapped a fresh roll of film into the camera and shot the crowd's reaction.

"Dane's here," Scott said, handing Jenna his clipboard.

As the motor home made a wide, ponderous turn into the RV lot we surged toward it like leaves in front of a blower. The driver's window rolled down, and a large hairy arm appeared, followed by a flat, wide face.

"Is this Texana's Trading Post?" asked the man who had pushed Dane Anthony's chair the night before. Several voices assured him it was.

Jose Reyes, standing beside me, said, "That rig must have cost more than the entire tax revenues of Presidio County. He must get some salary for that television show."

A portion of one side of the motor home opened, a section slid out, and a wheelchair lift, the same kind you see on buses and vans, lowered Dane Anthony, dressed in a buttery colored silk shirt and brown slacks. As soon as his wheelchair had rolled a few feet from the lift, he was surrounded by people saying hello and shaking his hand. In the middle of it all stood Jeremy Win, taking photo after photo.

The actor's driver stood in the background. The white knit shirt he wore revealed what last night's gray suit had not—a muscle-bound body that evoked thoughts of steroids and barbells. Embroidered in red script on the pocket was the name "Nellie." He did not look like a Nellie. His face, with its dented nose, brought to mind the boxing ring. Only his blue eyes, so serene they might never have seen anything unpleasant, were at odds with everything else about him. I wondered whether this was merely a physical curiosity or a manifestation of a state of mind.

At the front of the crowd, Scott said something to the actor, then looked around, caught my eye, and waved me over to be introduced. Up close, Dane Anthony was a striking man, pleasant to look at but ordinary enough not to intimidate. He might have been anybody's next-door neighbor. When he smiled, his eyes lit up; when he spoke, his voice was warm. He gripped my extended hand in both of his, brown eyes locked on mine.

"Texana, I'm so pleased to meet you again. I'm looking forward to a talk with you sometime soon. I was sorry to learn that your mother had died. Dear Sally was a very special person."

He gave my hand one last squeeze and released it. I felt a little jealous when he took Jenna's hand in turn. Then I saw the doglike look of adoration on her face and blushed at the certainty that my face bore the same look. I got out of there.

As I crossed the parking lot I saw Scott go inside the trading post. The tapings would be starting. I waved at Hap Boyer and Hugh Wesleco, who had avoided the group photograph but had been curious enough to show up. I went up the steps and took the chair next to Eva Ybarra, who waited with Jose Reyes and Gwen Masters.

Gwen had parked her silver LeSabre right in front of the porch, shortening the distance she had to walk with her new knee. She sat on the edge of one of my Corona Beer chairs, craning her neck to watch Dane Anthony, who had taken the truant Jimmy Ramos on his lap and was giving him a ride on the lift.

"I hate to see Dane come to this," she said sadly, sliding back in her chair.

"It's a lucky man who reaches *tercera edad* without infirmity," Jose said, who at seventy-one had reached the "third age" in robust health.

I could hear Scott's voice from inside as he issued instructions. Jenna came up the steps, smiled at us, and went inside only to come right back to announce that Scott was ready for

Mrs. Ybarra. Eva hoisted herself to her feet and went inside as Jenna held the door.

Across the lot, Nellie lifted Jimmy Ramos from the actor's lap, and the lift carried actor and chair up and into the RV. Nellie put the boy down, then went and unhooked the Pathfinder from the motor home and moved it to the far end of the RV lot. In the parking lot the Polveños moved to their cars and trucks, and the parking lot began to empty.

"Have you noticed?" Gwen said, waving her copy of the list at me to reclaim my attention. "They seem to be taking us according to age, oldest first. I guess they figure we may drop dead on 'em." She whooped with laughter that broke off abruptly when my husband's battered and worn green pickup pulled in near the gas pumps, sending gravel and dust flying. Clay was out of the door and moving toward the steps.

"Looks like something's wrong," Gwen said.

SIX

Where's Scott?" Clay said.

"Inside," I said. "But they're taping."

He halted in midstride, not looking pleased. "I need one of the videographers for a couple of hours."

"We'll go in the back way and ask Jenna," I said.

Walking beside Clay, matching him stride for stride, I asked no questions. I knew from his tight-lipped expression and the anger in his eyes that he was deeply upset. Whatever was wrong, I would find out when he spoke with Jenna.

We entered through the back door quietly. A wide hall connects our living quarters with the front. The double doors in between were open, and Jenna sat on a folding chair almost in the doorway, taking notes as Eva talked and the microphone and video camera recorded. Scott sat opposite Eva, smiling at her encouragingly as she spoke:

". . . Dane is one of the *buena gente*. That means 'good people.' Do you know that on the last day of the filming, after he had worked so many hours, he took time to come to my third daughter's *quinceañera*. That is, her fifteenth birthday party. This is a big event in our culture. Dane made it even more special for Felita. He even bought a gift. Felita treasures it to this day. . . ."

Jenna noticed Clay and me standing in the doorway. Obviously fearful that we would interrupt the videotaping, she left her post and came to where we stood, one finger pressed to her lips. We moved back into our quarters, taking Jenna with us. When the door closed, Clay didn't waste time or words.

"I've got a case of severe animal abuse. I need the horses' condition on videotape before the sheriff gets a court order to remove them. Could you spare the other videographer for this afternoon?"

Jenna, whose expression had changed from polite attention to genuine dismay at the mention of the animals' plight, wasted neither time nor words. Whispering, "Wait here," she slipped back down the hall and returned shortly with Chris. Clay explained what was needed. Chris agreed with such an air of tapped-down excitement that I decided he must thrive on the unexpected. He marched off to collect his equipment, saying he would meet us outside.

Clay went straight to the telephone and punched in a number. As soon as he started to speak, I realized that he'd called the sheriff. He described the situation once again, going into more detail than he had with Jenna and Chris. I couldn't tell from his expression, as he listened to the sheriff's response, whether Clay was getting any cooperation.

He hung up. "Tate will meet me there."

"Good. The situation sounds really bad," I said, as he collected a notebook and other items from the desk in the corner by the fireplace. "How'd you find out about it?"

"Jesse Waites hailed me on the road. He was walking in to find me. He spotted the horses early this morning while he was hunting."

"Poaching, you mean," I said. Jesse Waites is a character.

He lives in a ramshackle trailer on a site the Comanche would have approved for its fortress nature. His habit of hunting on other people's land isn't something ranchers condone, but because Jesse comes from a long-established local family, kills only enough for his needs, and never cuts fences, he is tolerated.

"I've got to fill up the gas tank again," Clay said, already halfway out the door. I went with him.

"You haven't seen the horses yourself?" I asked.

"No. Jesse's word is enough for me. He knows livestock, and he doesn't exaggerate. He says the animals are starved down to the bone."

Clay cut on the pump and pulled the hose as far as it would go in order to reach his pickup. In his hurry, he squeezed the handle too soon, spilling gas. Fumes rose around us.

"Who owns the horses?" I asked.

"Jesse didn't know the man's name," Clay said. "The horses are corralled on a hundred and forty acres somebody bought from Claude Neville up near Antelope Mountain."

Chris walked up, carrying a hand-held video camera and with a leather flight bag hanging from his shoulder. "Ready when you are," he said.

The pump cut off, and I took the nozzle and hose from Clay's hand so he could be on his way. Chris tossed his bag onto the seat and got into the pickup. Clay must have driven faster than usual. By the time I'd returned to the porch, his pickup was out of sight.

SEVEN

Everything all right?" Gwen said, as I sat down on the chair next to her.

I explained the situation because, sooner or later, she would hear about the neglected horses.

"I heard someone had bought acreage out that way, but I don't know who," Gwen said. "Do you, Jose?"

Jose shook his head, saying, "It'll be some newcomer. These city people show up, fall in love with the landscape, think they want to live here. They spend more on restoring some old adobe than the original owners made in a lifetime, brag to their friends about the peace and quiet, and when the new wears off, they're bored. Trouble is, they spend so much time doing, they've lost the art of enjoying."

"Jose, you're a philosopher," I said.

"If you ask me," Gwen said, "we need the newcomers. Ranching is a dying way of life. And the way this dry spell is going, the cows are going to have to graze at fifty miles an hour to get enough grass to stay alive."

The pair were still chewing over the subject when Eva Ybarra came out and said, "They want you next, Jose. I'm ready, Texana."

I told Eva I'd bring the pickup around. She'd ridden in with neighbors, and I'd promised to take her home. Eva had outlived two of her six children, and the others had moved away to find work. She lived alone.

It was a short drive down the road. Polvo is tucked in behind the outcrop of a mesa, so that you don't see it until you're there. A travel writer who had chanced the fifty-mile drive down the washboard road from Presidio had taken one look and turned around, later giving our community one sentence in his book on the Trans-Pecos: "A hot, dreary little place full of barking cur dogs." It's true that the adobes are the color of the dust that mounds in the road, the trailers have a tired look, and the dogs are scruffy mutts that scratch a lot and bark even more, but on a clear day the sky above is pale turquoise, the dust motes turn the harsh sunlight golden, and the shadows of mesquite leaves dance in the wind and make patterns against the walls of the houses that are home to families, with names like Risa and Luna and Ybarra, who, on the stones in the cemetery, can trace their history back to 1879. I know every family, down to the names of their dogs. Except for my years away at college and a brief first marriage, I'd known nothing but this place and these people. I saw Polvo with eyes of affection and familiarity.

I stopped in front of the Ybarra house. Eva gave me a searching look, one hand on the pickup door. "I liked your mother. I was thinking this morning how like her you are. She was a good person, a friend to many. You look like your father, but in your ways you're so like her."

As she stepped down, there was a muffled boom. Eva looked back at me. "What was that?"

I twisted around in my seat trying to determine the direction of the echoing sound. "If I didn't know better, I'd say the highway engineers were still trying to blast a way through the rimrock for the road above," I said.

Eva slammed the truck door. "Ha! Everybody here told them that roadwork beyond here would just wash out, but they wouldn't listen. All that money wasted and still no road extension."

She gave me a last wave and went inside. I made a wide U-turn at the school bus turnaround, driving back through Polvo quickly, worried about that unexplained explosive noise.

When I made the curve in the road around the mesa, I saw black smoke spinning upward above the treetops, thinning as it rose.

EIGHT

In the RV lot, all that was left of Dane Anthony's motor home was a jagged metal frame, like a giant sardine can peeled open.

For yards in every direction the ground was littered with clumps of burning debris, like hundreds of small campfires.

Amid the rubble, Jenna clung to Scott's side, her head buried in his shoulder. Jose Reyes knelt at their feet, trying to help Ben, who lay on the ground.

I stopped at the edge of the road, got out, and ran to them. Ben's face and neck were flecked with blood, but it was his arm that was the cause of the pain contorting his face.

Scott, his voice shaking, said, "I think the fire extinguisher hit him when the explosion blew it out of my hands."

Scott didn't look too well himself. His face was dotted with bleeding nicks, and his torn shirt was stained from the cuts to his chest and arms.

Jeremy appeared, a clean shirt in one hand, a long metal tray in the other. Kneeling by Ben, he persuaded the videographer to let Jose support the broken arm. Then he used the shirt and the tray as a makeshift splint.

"We need help over here!"

Dane Anthony had shouted from the porch of the trading post. I asked Jenna if she was hurt, but she was beyond hearing me. I took her by the arms, expecting a struggle, but she let go of Scott, clutched at me, and allowed me to lead her away. As we reached the steps, Nellie came out of the trading post with a dog leash, one of the soft fabric ones I sell. Gwen lay on the porch, deathly white, one arm stretched up to Dane Anthony, who held her hand in both of his.

Gwen's dark slacks were darker still on one leg from the blood that pulsed out around the protruding metal fragment. Nellie knelt beside her, put his hand on her shoulder, and said, "I'm Nelson Kalganov. I'm a licensed nurse."

He looped the leash around Gwen's leg above the knee and tied it off, then he put one finger under the tourniquet. "Making sure it isn't too tight," he said.

Gwen, her expression truly scared for the first time since I'd known her, nonetheless looked up at me and said, "My new knee. It's not paid for yet."

"I think you should ask the doctor for a refund, my dear," Dane Anthony said.

I got Jenna into a chair and rushed inside to call for help. Odessa, with the nearest Medivac unit, was two hundred miles away, over two hours' flight time for the helicopter. The Border Patrol and state troopers would come, but their helicopters, even if already airborne, wouldn't be as quick as what I had in mind.

I dialed the number from memory and said a silent prayer that someone would be home. A gruff "Hello." I explained what was needed.

I went to tell Gwen that George Hawkins was on the way.

"Smart thinking," Gwen said, relief showing in her eyes.

"Is he a doctor?" Dane Anthony asked.

"Rancher," I said. "With a helicopter. He's only fourteen

miles upriver. It's the fastest way to get her to the regional hospital in Alpine."

Scott, Jose, and Jeremy, supporting Ben, reached the steps. Ben gave a little moan as they eased him into a chair.

"Gwen, what's your blood type so I can alert the hospital?" I asked.

"B positive. They typed it before the knee surgery."

Nellie was speaking soothingly to Jenna. As I went back inside he was right behind me, propelling Jenna in front of him. While I called the hospital, Nellie guided Jenna to the couch. While I talked to the emergency room nurse, he heated water in the microwave.

As I hung up he was stirring spoonfuls of sugar into the pot of instant coffee. Efficiently, he put cups on a tray, filled them, and carried one to Jenna and told her to drink it. He carried the tray to the porch as I followed.

As we stepped out the door I heard the droning helicopter, and in an instant it was dipping toward us, setting down on the road, its rotor blade sending debris from the blast flying. Nellie put the tray down on the table by the door.

"I'm going to lift her," he said. Then to Jose and me: "The two of you support her leg. Try to keep it level. On the count of three. One . . . two . . . three."

Gwen gave a muffled groan as he scooped her into his arms and Jose and I lifted her leg. It was awkward, but we got her to the helicopter.

George Hawkins reached across from the right side, where the command seat was, and slid open the door. Nellie, as big as he was, managed to get in with Gwen on the backseat and cradle her on his lap, which helped take the pressure off her knee. I stepped back and out of the way as Jeremy helped Ben into the left front seat beside the pilot, then slid the door closed.

Jeremy, Jose, and I moved off. The revolutions of the rotor blade increased to an invisible whirl, and the helicopter soared upward, flying northeast. Only then did I notice the water truck that was stopped farther along the road, waiting for the helicopter to take off. Red light revolving, the tanker rolled slowly forward, turning into the RV lot. Behind it came a pickup, the bed overflowing with people. Someone in Polvo had seen the smoke rising from behind the mesa and alerted the volunteers by ringing the triangle hanging in front of the post office.

The pickup parked beside the water truck next to the smoldering remains of the RV. Three men and a woman efficiently managed the hose and pump, and a hiss of white steam went up as the water hit the hot metal frame. The other volunteers put out the burning piles with shovels and burlap bags.

As the volunteers sprayed water from one end of the destroyed motor home to the other, Jeremy and I walked back to the porch. Scott, assuring me that his cuts were superficial, asked me where he could wash the blood off his face.

"When is the last time you had a tetanus shot?" I asked, thinking of the many animals that had been through Clay's pens and the force of the blast that might have driven contaminated dirt into Scott's cuts.

He looked at me blankly. "I don't know."

I persuaded Scott to go into Presidio to see the nurse who ran the family health clinic by saying it would make Jenna feel better if he was checked over. Jose offered to drive him, but Scott insisted on driving himself. Jenna insisted on going along. After the pair left, I collapsed into a chair with no certainty that I could rise immediately if needed.

Dane Anthony rolled his wheelchair over to me with the last cup of coffee from the tray and placed it in my hands, suggesting I drink it, as I looked a "trifle pale." I was going to take his advice, but then I saw Jeremy Win's ashen face and gave the last cup to him.

NINE

By six I had showered and washed the sooty smell from my hair, changed into fresh clothes, and answered a half-dozen telephone calls from concerned and curious friends that inevitably began, "I hear you had a little excitement at your place." The last had been from Hugh Wesleco, and it was a measure of my mental and emotional fatigue that I forgot to tell him about Gwen.

I had poured myself a whiskey and settled in the rocking chair by the fireplace when Clay came in looking bewildered and apprehensive.

"Are you all right? What happened out there? Whose RV was that?"

"I'm okay." I raised my glass. "Join me and I'll tell you about it. Isn't Chris with you?"

"He's talking to Jeremy."

Clay poured his drink and sat down in the twin rocker

opposite mine. After I told him how my day had gone, he asked how Gwen was.

"I called the hospital about an hour ago. She was still in surgery. The same doctor will be setting the fracture on Ben's arm in the morning."

"But what caused the explosion?" Clay asked.

"The propane for the RV's cooktop and grill. Juan Risas talked to me after he and the other volunteers got things dampened down. Somehow the RV caught fire inside. The heat expanded the gas in the cylinders until they blew up like bombs and turned the motor home into shrapnel. Did you see the mesquite by your office with the chunk of metal embedded in the trunk? Well, the same effect is what nearly took off Gwen's leg."

"How'd it happen?" Clay said.

"Dane and Nellie said there was nothing wrong when they left the RV for the trading post. Nellie went in to watch the taping session. Dane stayed on the porch with Gwen. They heard a popping sound, saw smoke coming out the RV's windows. Dane yelled for the others. Scott came running out with the fire extinguisher. Ben was right behind him. Jeremy had stopped to help Jose take the mike off. Then the RV blew up. Juan said it could have been burning for as little as ten minutes. Apparently RVs are made of everything flammable."

Clay looked at me sharply. "What caused the fire?"

"Juan said he smelled gasoline in the ashes, but that could have been from the RV's tank. It's up to the State Fire Marshal's Office to send an investigator. Juan said we should leave everything just as it is until Dane's insurance company is notified. The volunteers cleaned up enough of the parking lot for people to drive in, but they bagged and tagged everything and put it all in our shed in case it's needed."

"The insurance company will want an investigation," Clay said. "Especially since people were injured."

"One of the clinic windows took a direct hit. We'll have to put a board or some plastic over it," I said.

Clay was no longer listening. His face had hardened into the question that neither of us could answer. Was the fire in any way connected to the anonymous note?

He stood up. "I think I need a touch more whiskey. You?" I shook my head.

"Was Rosalinda Pray here, too, when it happened?" Clay asked as he sat back down with a full glass.

"According to Scott, she's rented the Alstons' guest house for two weeks and hired one of their ranch hands to play chauffeur. And she brought a maid along. I guess so there's someone to clean up after the dog. Did you know it peed on Scott at the party?"

"Jack Russell terriers do that when they're excited. They're nervy dogs."

"It's a good thing Rosalinda and pet weren't here then. Doggy would have shit its little brains out over today's excitement," I said. "Nellie and Jeremy certainly kept their heads."

"Who's Nellie?"

"Dane's nurse. The man behind the wheelchair last night." I explained how he had saved Gwen from bleeding to death. "He went to the hospital with her. George Hawkins flew him back."

"Where are they staying, this Nellie and his boss, now that the RV's gone?"

"In Scott and Jenna's RV. I replaced some of their lost clothes with things from my stock. As soon as Dane is rested, he'll probably get into his Pathfinder and drive straight back to Los Angeles. What a welcome! He'll probably sue us. I wonder if he thinks we have enough to be suable? Is that a word?"

"Let's hope not," he said drily.

"How'd it go with the horses?" I asked.

"Sheriff Tate was as good as his word. I think he was more shocked than he cared to admit over their condition." Clay checked his watch. "He'll have the court order to seize them by now. He's meeting me back at the barn first thing in the morning."

"Excuse me." Chris stood in the doorway between the front room and our quarters. I told him to come in and sit down. Clay offered him whiskey, which he declined.

"I need to call the people who were supposed to be video-taped tomorrow and cancel," he said, "but my cell phone doesn't seem to work."

"You're about a hundred miles from the nearest cell," Clay told him.

"You don't need to worry about notifying anyone," I said, smiling at the thought. "They'll all know by now. This is big country, but it's a small world."

The telephone rang, and I went to the extension in the bed-room, thinking it would be another neighbor.

It was Scott, asking if I would let Chris know that he and Jenna had checked into the Three Palms Inn in Presidio for the night. "We're going into Alpine in the morning to see Ben and buy some clothes for Dane," he added. "It will be late after-noon before we get back."

When I rejoined Clay and Chris, they were discussing the horses. "Chris wants to videotape the rescue," Clay said.

"I think you're clear for time," I said, giving him Scott's message.

"Great," Chris said. "I'll go with you then. What I'd really like to do is follow the progress of the horses. How long before they're back to normal?"

"Six months to a year," Clay said. "But there's no guar-antee of a happy ending. When animals have been as neglected as these, anything can go wrong anytime."

"How soon before they show some improvement?" Chris asked.

"Probably six weeks."

"So I could tape them in six weeks, then at six months. It's really powerful stuff we got today. If I follow it up and the ending is happy, it'll make a great short documentary. I told Jere he should come along and take stills."

"We leave at seven," Clay said, getting to his feet. "Right

now I've got to make some arrangements for tomorrow." He crossed to the door and was gone.

Chris said good-night. I offered to make sandwiches, but he said there was plenty of food in the RV's refrigerator and Nellie had offered to cook.

After he'd gone, I heated leftover stew. When Clay didn't come in after forty minutes, I walked out to the clinic. He was at his desk in the office off the waiting room.

"Did you make your calls?" I asked.

"Hugh Wesleco's sending me a couple of his ranch hands and a trailer to transport the horses to Cinco's place."

"Do you think you can save them?"

"I won't know until I examine them, but if anybody can keep those horses alive, it's Cinco."

TEN

A chill mist rose off the river, frost sheathed the low grasses, and the coming dawn wrapped the eastern horizon with a red rim as Clay and I loaded bales of alfalfa hay from the shed into my pickup. By the time we'd moved Clay's truck into place, Chris had appeared. He stowed his gear in the cab and helped us load a half-ton of sweet feed in fifty-pound bags. Clay went to get his medicine case, and we were ready. Except for Jeremy. Just when I thought Clay would send Chris to get him, the photographer came bounding out of his trailer, camera case in hand, his jacket half on, pockets bulging with film cartridges.

Chris rode with Clay, while Jeremy followed in his Suburban. I brought up the rear. We drove north along a ranch road that climbed into the rolling plains and grasslands known as the Marfa Highlands. The cold nights had long since turned the grama grasses golden. The treeless landscape was dotted with jutting maguey stalks, and the blue of the Chinati Mountains rode the horizon, the whole framed by an immensity of sky.

To reach our destination, we passed through a ranch that comprised twenty sections. The only break in the flow of grasses was a barbed-wire fence stretching across the miles.

At the far boundary we rumbled across a pipe cattleguard, disturbing the grazing of nine pronghorn antelopes. At the sound of our approach they lifted their deerlike heads, turned their white rumps toward us, and bolted. Five miles farther, our caravan of vehicles turned due east onto a track that was little better than two narrow ruts ending at a board-and-batten cedar cabin constructed so recently that the wood still retained its golden color.

Past the house stood a barn, its wood grayed with age. It had been the work of an earlier generation of builders. The adjoining corral, like the cabin, looked new.

The two men talking together beside the Sheriff's Department Grand Marquis turned their heads expectantly in our direction as we parked alongside the '88 Silvarado towing a well-used horse trailer.

Sheriff Skeeter Tate welcomed us with a raised hand. The man beside him gave no sign of welcome. Nasario Arias, "Cinco" to his friends, conserved himself in gesture as well as word, saving his energies for the abused horses, ponies, and mules that he devoted his time and money to rehabilitating. A small man, he wore a thick, plaid shirt, well-worn jeans, round-toed work boots, and a red Texas Rangers baseball cap.

As we were getting out of our vehicles two more pickups, one towing an open-top trailer, drove up. Hugh Wesleco's ranch hands, Gus and Jake, had arrived. Chris captured them with the hand-held video camera as they got out of their vehicle. Jeremy pulled a roll of film from one pocket and loaded it.

Clay made introductions. Beyond that, no one said much. In the face of the sight in front of us, words seemed pointless. As a vet's wife, I face the reality of humans' maltreatment of animals on a regular basis, but I have never become inured to it.

The four bony horses inside the corral looked back at us with lusterless eyes and drooping heads. Their coats, dulled by malnutrition, were so dry the hair stood up in tufts. Their hooves were overgrown, curling up six or seven inches.

Jake uttered a low oath. "Good thing Jesse reported them to you when he did. Look at this corral, the wires all stretched out where they shoved their heads through, trying to get at the grass out here."

"There's a pony trapped in one stall," Cinco said.

"How bad is it?" Clay asked.

"The roof fell in on it. It's pinned, but its head is still up."

Clay, his medicine case in one hand, opened the gate and let it swing wide. "No need to close it," he said. "These animals aren't going anywhere without help."

"I'll back the trailer into position," Jake said.

As we filed into the corral behind Clay I pulled on cowhide work gloves and took in details: empty feed trough, one barrel of scummy water, rock-hard ground.

Talking softly and soothingly, a soft halter ready in his hands, Cinco approached the closest horse, a mare, and slipped the halter over her head. He stroked her muzzle and neck, talking to her softly, while Clay started his examination. The other three horses remained perfectly still, without visible fear or interest.

Chris had started taping at the opening of the gate. Jeremy, camera in hand, stood next to me, watching intently. "What exactly is Clay doing?"

"Looking for soft-tissue injuries, broken bones, abscesses, things like that. He'll give a vitamin injection, another for worms. Then he'll pull blood for testing."

When Clay had satisfied himself as to the condition of the first mare, he moved to another that Jake had haltered.

Then it was time for the rest of us to do our jobs. With Cinco still at the mare's head, Gus, the sheriff, and I positioned ourselves at her sides. Cinco pulled on the halter firmly, but she balked and dug in her heels. Gus moved to her rump, applied his shoulder, and pushed. Jake came to help. We worked the mare toward the trailer by slow increments, pushing, hauling, then resting the creature, which trembled from the exertion. When we reached the low ramp of the trailer, Cinco had to lift first one then the other of the mare's front feet onto the ramp. Both he and Jake pulled at the halter while Gus and I pushed from behind. Finally, we worked her into the trailer, where we stacked bales of hay around her so she could not fall. The mare nibbled at the hay.

Sweating from the exertion, we shed our jackets before tackling the next horse. It was a slow, exhausting process, but after several hours we had all four animals loaded, two per trailer. Jake and Gus left for Cinco's. They would unload the horses, put out feed and water, and return.

Cinco, Clay, the sheriff, and I went to work removing the fallen boards that had pinned the pony inside the stall. Chris recorded our progress. Jeremy put his camera in the pickup and came to help us. We worked silently for the most part. The brown pony inside watched us with nervous eyes. It could not know we were there to help.

When the last board was cleared, Clay checked over the pony, a gelding. "He's badly dehydrated. Let's try and get him on his feet."

We tried, but the pony could not help us, so we had to rig a pulley, using rope and a blanket under his belly. Once he was up, we had to support him to keep him that way. Still, it was a victory.

"This is the worst thing I've ever seen, and the best thing I've ever done," Jeremy said, his face immeasurably sad.

When Jake and Gus returned, it took all of us to load the pony into Cinco's trailer. Then the ranch hands left for home and the sheriff left for Marfa. We still had to get the pony to Cinco's and unload all the feed.

We made the twelve-mile drive slowly to give the pony an easy ride. The modesty of Cinco's stucco ranch house was offset by the spectacular surroundings, a flat plain between jutting limestone mountains. The barn had an adjoining series of corrals designed to keep sick or contagious equines separate but in sight of other animals so they would not feel lonely.

The pony unloaded easily and made his way on shaky legs into a stall. Cinco hung buckets of fresh water and feed over the door. I was so used to Chris and his video camera and Jeremy with his camera that I forgot they were there. Clay set up the IV that Cinco would oversee for the six to eight hours it would take to fully rehydrate the pony. After that, we unloaded the bales of alfalfa hay and the sacks of sweet feed into the barn. I broke open a bale and scattered it in the trough. Cinco followed along behind me pouring a liquid vitamin supplement over the hay. Last, Clay took a blood sample from the pony and squeezed a full tube of a paste antibiotic down his throat to heal his pressure sores. We made our way into the shade of the barn's overhang. Clay put his medicine case on the work table and opened it.

"I'm leaving some things with you, Cinco."

He set out on the table three fourteen-gauge, two-inch needles for intravenous therapy, extra IV simplex hose, three tubes of Bute and three of antiseptic cream, and two amber bottles and a box of sixteen-gauge needles that he put to one side.

"This," Clay said, tapping the bottles, "is a new antibiotic for shipping fever in cattle. Try it on those Mexican steers you bought. It's supposed to be effective on the resistant cases. Just remember, it's for cattle only. It's fatal to horses." Clay closed the case, then added, "Don't use an automatic pump syringe. If it accidently pumps the stuff into a vein, it's deadly, even in the cattle. And don't stick yourself either, or we'll be burying you."

"Can that really happen?" Chris asked me. "Accidentally injecting yourself?" Jeremy leaned in to listen to my answer.

"More often than you might think," I said. "Livestock don't understand the words 'keep still.' I once wormed my thumb instead of a cow."

Cinco and Clay were still talking as we went to our vehicles. In front of them, Chris walked backward to capture the scene. I went to my truck and got in, starting the motor as a hint to my husband. Jeremy came running up with his camera to snap Cinco and Clay as they leaned on the pickup discussing the ongoing care of the horses. Finally, the pair shook hands and we were under way.

My growling stomach told me it was long past lunch. I was dirty and tired, and I smelled of horse. I followed Clay's truck, driving without paying attention to the familiar route. It seemed a long way home.

Jeremy turned in at the RV lot and stopped beside his trailer. In the parking lot the late afternoon sun gleamed on Gwen's Buick and the blue Suburban beside it with Ned Farmer, the Alstons' ranch hand, behind the wheel. He lifted his eyes to the rearview mirror as we turned in and raised a hand in a lazy greeting. Clay drove past straight to the back.

I stopped, stepped out of the pickup, walked over to the vehicle, and leaned in at the passenger side. "We're closed, but—"

"You're not leaving this dip-shit place until I say so." The woman's shrill voice carried like a coach's whistle. I looked around and saw Rosalinda Pray coming out of Scott's RV. Her face was flushed, and her mouth was so tight it would have taken a pry bar to open it. She was walking fast in my direction.

"It's all right," Ned said to me. "I'm just waiting on the lady. And may I say, it's a pure pleasure." He laughed without humor.

By the time she reached me, Rosalinda Pray was smiling. I compared the lean and hungry-looking woman before me to her youthful image captured in my mother's photographs. Her face held a memory of that beauty, but her body had been dieted down to an unnatural thinness, and beneath the flawless makeup the line of her jaw was too tight, the unlined forehead too smooth, and the pouting lips too full. I expected the plastic surgery stitches to give way, the botox injections to wear off, and the collagen beneath the skin to collapse, leaving her like a deflated balloon.

"You must be . . . the trading post person," she said brightly. "I came as soon as I heard what happened. I had to see with my own eyes that Dane was all right."

She got into the Suburban and leaned back against the seat. "We can go now," she said to the driver. He winked at me and started the motor.

"Nice to meet you," I said as they drove away.

ELEVEN

I sank into a chair at the breakfast table. "I didn't sleep worth a damn. We need a new mattress. Ours is so saggy I feel like I'm sleeping in a hole."

"If you think we need one, buy one," Clay said, giving me a wary look over his coffee cup.

"I hate it when you do that."

He shifted in his chair, refusing to make eye contact, like a kid trying to read crib notes with the teacher standing over him.

"Agree with you?"

"Humor me."

"Are you feeling bad?"

"I'm just tired."

Clay gulped the last of his coffee and got up, leaving most of his breakfast on the plate. "I'll be in the clinic doing the paperwork on those blood samples."

As the back door closed behind him, I rubbed my head and felt guilty, which made me still more irritable. I knew exactly what was bothering me. I was more than tired, I was exhausted, a reaction to the past two days. I no longer bounced back from emotional stress or physical exertion as quickly as I once did.

I carried the dishes to the kitchen and scraped the remains of eggs and toast into the trash bin, then ran water in the sink. Life was one load of dirty dishes after another.

As I rinsed the skillet I thought about the rest of my mother's things waiting in the top of the closet. I went to the bedroom, taking the stepladder with me.

I put aside the two remaining family albums to look at later. As I opened the second box I smelled roses, my mother's fragrance. I lifted the contents, things I had chosen from among her possessions to keep, put away for so long I had forgotten them: a silk scarf the color of the sky; a pair of white kid gloves two sizes too small for my hands; a large pink and white seashell; a lock of her hair, brown and glossy, tied with a thin ribbon. I touched it and remembered how, every spring when the weather turned hot, she would cut her hair short. Next came a leatherbound book of poetry inscribed "To Sally from Grandmother" on the title page; a perfume bottle with a glass rose stopper; and a fifth-anniversary card from my father in which he had written "To my darling girl" over the printed message. In the very bottom of the box was a flat, tissue-wrapped parcel, stiff like a thin book and tied with a green ribbon. I had no memory of ever having packed it, though I must have.

I unfolded the yellowing tissue and found a clothbound notebook, filled with my mother's handwriting. A kind of journal. Dated 1961. I read half a sentence before Clay called my name.

He was standing by the kitchen table, on which sat a deep cardboard box.

"I'm going into Marfa to ship the blood samples to the lab," he said. "This is the rest of the new antibiotic. Ten bottles. You can put them with the other vet supplies out front anytime you like."

The trip to Marfa and back would take most of the day. I was about to ask him to wait until I made out a grocery list—I sell only canned and packaged goods and have to shop, like everyone else, for fresh produce—but Jenna came in.

"We've rescheduled the tapings we missed. May I use the telephone to notify people?"

Clay was going out the door as I handed her the Big Bend telephone book. "Will Dane be staying?" I asked her.

She nodded. "Scott and I moved our things into the office with Chris. Ben's going back to Austin as soon as he gets out of the hospital, so there's room. A bit tight, but room."

"I see." I reminded her that about three-fourths of Polvo wasn't in the telephone book. "Tell Lucy at the post office. She'll pass the word to anyone you can't reach."

I picked up the box of antibiotic and went through to the front. As soon as Scott saw me he asked if he could salvage some time by videotaping me. His face looked as if he'd been shaved by a mad barber. The cuts from the explosion had scabbed over but were still raw-looking.

I placed the multi-dose bottles on the shelves with other veterinary products—tetracycline, wound spray, iodine, various sizes of hypodermic needles and syringes, betadine cleansing solution, latex gloves, and Vet wrap. Then I went to hastily apply some makeup to the circles under my eyes.

When I was ready, Scott clipped a small microphone on my collar. "Sit all the way back and keep both feet flat on the floor," he said. "Look at me, not the camera. I'll ask a few warm-up questions to get you relaxed. Speak in your normal tone. We'll adjust the sound recording to you. First, take a deep breath and hold it for a few seconds."

Scott was a good interviewer. By his fourth question I had stopped thinking about the video camera.

"Did you have a favorite among the stars?" he said.

"Rosalinda Pray."

"Why was she your favorite?"

"She's behind you."

Scott half-twisted around in his chair, then rose to his feet. When he saw that the actress had brought her dog along, he gave a sad good-bye glance down at his suede shoes before stepping forward to greet her.

"Your poor face," she said. "Did the explosion do that?"

Scott said, "Superficial nicks." He ushered her over to me. I stood, not considering the previous night's meeting a formal introduction.

"So you were one of the movie extras," she said. "It was a very exciting time, wasn't it?"

The dog squirmed in her arms. "You want down, sweetie?" She put the dog on the floor. It ran across the room, leaving a wet trail that the worn floorboards rapidly soaked up.

"Pippa always does that in an unfamiliar place. She has simply ruined the rug in the Alstons' guest house at the ranch," Rosalinda Pray said, in a tone that implied it was cute.

"Clever dog," I said.

Rosalinda straightened her back. "What?"

"Able to run and pee at the same time."

Jeremy walked in, and she hugged him. Scott offered her his chair. She put her hands on the back and leaned on it. She was squeezed into jeans so tight that sitting might have been problematic. But no amount of dieting could turn back the clock on body shape.

The majority of Rosalinda Pray's portion of the video, Scott explained to me, had been taped at her home in California, so she had met the crew already. "Of course, she's known Jeremy since he was a kid," he added, then turned to the actress.

"I met with Dane yesterday," Rosalinda said. "We're in complete agreement that what this project needs is publicity. So we've hired a publicist."

"A publicist?" Scott's eyes widened.

"To create anticipation. This fire is the perfect opportunity. The publicist will get the word out about Pancho Villa's curse striking again—"

"What curse?" Scott asked.

"During the filming the *villista* was murdered. Right before the premiere, Rudolf drove into a bridge abutment. Jon French died of a stroke. Your little video project is barely under way and my co-star narrowly escapes an explosion. A curse follows anything to do with *Panchito*. Just like Macbeth."

"Or the curse of Pharaoh," Chris said under his breath, detaching me from the microphone. My taping was obviously over.

Scott gave a strained smile. "Rosalinda, this is PBS, not—"

"Not *what?*" Her voice held a warning.

Before Scott could say "soap opera" or "tabloid," Jeremy saved him. "Sounds like this might be a good way to broaden the video's viewer base."

"I knew I could count on you," Rosalinda Pray smiled up at Jeremy. "Go and tell Dane I'm here, will you?" As the photographer headed obediently for the door, she turned back to Scott. "I have some suggestions about my lines for the taping at the location site."

The dog had completed her investigation of the premises and circled back to sit at Rosalinda's feet. She gave a whining bark. Rosalinda Pray placed a manicured hand under her pet's chin. "Hungries? Chris, be a dear and bring me the canvas bag from the car. Pippa's snacks are in it."

Chris hurried out. Scott was consulting his clipboard and asking the actress what time she would be available the next day. More rescheduling for Scott and telephoning for Jenna. I decided I could escape without being noticed.

Jenna was hanging up the telephone receiver as I walked in. I told her Rosalinda Pray had arrived. She made a face and struck a line through a name on her list, sighed, and said, "I guess I'd better go and say hello." She went through to the front, and I got out the coffee and the filters.

The twelve-cup coffeemaker had given a last gurgle and the pot was filled when someone shouted shrilly, "Do something!"

TWELVE

Jenna burst in. "She's choking!"

"Rosalinda?"

"The dog," she said frantically. "Where's Clay?"

I was already moving as I said, "Clay's not here."

In the front, Chris and Scott knelt by the little dog, which lay on the floor. Nearby was a small bag of dried dog food, its contents spilled. Rosalinda Pray stood over her pet, saying, "Do something. Help her."

Seeing me, the two men moved aside. I got on my knees beside the dog. Her eyes were already glassy and a little foam flicked her mouth.

I'd seen my husband do what I was about to attempt more than once, but the feel of that small, warm body in my hands almost unnerved me. With one hand under the dog's hindquarters, I elevated her rear while feeling for her diaphragm with my other hand. Using two fingers, I gave a quick firm push. Nothing. Again. A gluey mass shot out of her mouth onto the floor.

"I'd suggest canned dog food from now on," I said, handing the dog to her tearful owner. I went and got a paper towel, picked up the gob of food, and threw it in the trash behind the counter.

Rosalinda Pray cuddled the dog like a baby and made kissy sounds. Chris patted me on the back. Scott said, "I was afraid to touch it." Jenna hugged me around the waist.

Jeremy came in the front door. "Nellie says Dane's not feeling well. . . . Is everything all right?"

Rosalinda kept her cheek pressed to the dog's head. "Pippa nearly died while this bunch stood around with their thumbs up their butts." She turned blue eyes on me. "You saved my Pippi. I want you to call me Rosy."

I said I had prepared coffee. "Lovely," she said. "We'll have a nice chat. Just you and me." I had meant the invitation for everyone, but Scott looked relieved.

Rosalinda followed me through to the back, then looked around with some curiosity at the room. Despite the tight pants, she managed to sit on the couch with the dog in her lap. But the doggy had a mind of her own and moved over to rest against the cushions. I could only hope she wouldn't get excited.

I put two cups on the tray, poured the coffee, and carried it to the coffee table. "Do you take cream or sugar?"

"I'll take it Irish, if you have any whiskey." I got the bottle and tipped in a measure. She was looking at the album, still open to the photograph of her and Dane with the *villista.*

Rosalinda took her cup, sipped, then reached for more whiskey. The dog had stretched out and closed her eyes. The actress looked so tired I thought she might do the same. She drank some more coffee. "That's better," she said, suddenly alert and watching me.

"Would you like something to eat with that?" I asked, half-rising from the armchair. "I've got cookies. Or I can make you a sandwich."

"The whiskey has all the calories I can afford," she said. I sat down. "Do you have to diet?"

"Not really. I take after my father."

"It's all metabolism. My fourth husband burned calories sitting on the couch. It was his only talent." She turned up her cup and emptied it, then set it on the coffee table next to the album.

"You didn't see me at my best yesterday," she said. "I've known Dane forever. We fight but we make up. I persuaded him to agree to this project. Do you know why? The last time I was offered a part in a film was nineteen eighty-two. One of those Burt Reynolds trucker horrors. They wanted me to play his mother. Fine, I said. Then I read the script. Straight man to one of those hairy red monkeys. That was my part."

"Orangutan?"

"What?"

"The monkey. Ape. I think I have that movie in video rental. Wasn't it an orangutan?"

"How the hell should I know? The point I was trying to make is that this project is a stepping-stone. A chance for some decent exposure for me. Television. That's the place for a mature actor. Dane has found his place in the spotlight. Now its my turn."

The dog raised her head and looked lovingly at her mistress. Rosalinda touched her head. "Feeling better, baby?" She stroked the dog absently, her eyes going back to the photograph in the album.

"Jacinto was a handsome man," she said. "Not tall, but he carried himself as if he was. He had wonderful eyes, full of compassion. And danger. Too bad I never had the chance to put him in my autobiography."

"Your autobiography?" I said. I realized my thoughtlessness too late. She caught me blushing and laughed. "Never heard of it? Well, not many people did. *Pray Tell.* That was the title. All about my seven husbands and a few special friends. Sales were dismal. I should have acted with the damn monkey. Like I said, Jacinto was attractive. I'd have invited him into my trailer on the set anytime."

"What stopped you?"

"Jon French. Before the filming started, he read me the riot act. Tiresome man. 'You have a capacity for love, Rosy. Please don't exercise it during the shoot, especially with the locals.' "

"But I thought—" I stopped.

"My hot romance with Dane?" she said, a laugh in her voice. "A publicity stunt. Jon came up with the idea. That's partly why he wanted me on my best behavior. Not that I didn't enjoy flirting with my co-star. Dane was attractive and charming. I wouldn't have objected to more than a flirtation. But Dane wasn't interested in personally charming me any more than Jacinto was. Of course, Jacinto might have found time for me if he hadn't fallen for one of the locals. Sally, that was her name. A little brunette who—"

It was Rosalinda's turn to blush.

"Ran the trading post," I said quietly.

"Have I made a dreadful faux pas? Was she a relation?"

"My mother."

"Your mother?" she said. "I would never have guessed. You don't look a thing like her. Anyway, it was just friendly, I'm sure. He admired her." She picked up the dog and stood. "My hosts, the Alstons, are giving a small dinner party for me tonight, and I have a million things to attend to." She cradled the dog closer and walked briskly down the shallow hall and through to the front. I heard her saying good-bye to Scott and the others, and then it was quiet.

I sat the cups back on the tray. The couch had a wet stain where the dog had been. I scrubbed at it with paper towels and disinfectant, then put the cushion out in the sun to dry.

I returned to the bedroom, closed the door against disturbance, and picked up my mother's journal.

THIRTEEN

I sat curled up on the couch, the family album in my lap, staring down at the last photograph on the last page, one taken by my friend Maria. In it, my parents and I stood in front of the secondhand Pontiac they bought for me to drive to college. We wore our best faces like Sunday clothes. The picture showed no trace of the chronic depression that blighted my father's life, or of my mother's constant anxiety for him.

My father had arranged for the car by calling on one of his many friends from the days before his illness made him a recluse. The Pontiac arrived with new paint, new upholstery, and an overhauled engine. Always, my mother had given me love without limit, comfort after skinned knees, patient help with my homework. But it had been my father who had chosen all my birthday and Christmas gifts, seeming to understand exactly what I wanted without being told, for I had never been a vocal child, nor one much aware of the world beyond the border. He had given me books in countless number, antique furniture for my room, paintings and photographs for the walls. He had formed my tastes and exposed me to a world beyond my own. I had loved both my parents equally. I had taken for granted that their love for each other was equal.

Clay came in. "I went by Cinco's. The pony is improved since the IV. He just may make it." He washed his hands at the sink, then came around the couch to join me. "Are you blue?" he said, as he caught sight of my face.

"My mother had a love affair with Jacinto Trejo."

"The *villista*? Who told you that?"

I put the album aside and held up the bound notebook. "It's here. This is a journal she kept about the movie days. About herself, really. Pour me a whiskey, will you?"

Clay was silent for a moment, then poured us each a drink and sat down in the chair facing me. "Tell me," he said, handing me a glass.

"The entries begin in February, when the movie producer came to see the location sites his scouts had chosen. I guess she intended to record everything about the moviemaking. This is what she wrote on February fifth."

> Jon French and three other men came to the trading post to meet Justice and see the place on our land where they intend to build a set. Justice drove them. His spirits are better. He seems almost like his old self. Jon French liked the spot instantly and offered a payment that Justice thought very fair since we don't use the land. They stayed for dinner. One of the men, Jacinto Trejo, actually rode with Pancho Villa. Like so many in Mexico, he has no idea of the date of his birth, but thinks he was about ten when he joined the revolutionaries. One of Villa's captains pointed a rifle at his chest and asked if he wanted to be a soldier. His stories about Villa kept

> us entertained over dinner. He and Jon French seem to get along well.

"She mentions Trejo a few more times, but not consistently until the filming actually begins. Before that, there are pages about something she calls a photographic-interview-social-research team that arrived in late February, and later a lot about the six weeks of construction." I turned to the next page I had folded back to mark the sequence of the relationship.

> Mr. French was pleased. Construction costs are well below estimates. He credits Jacinto Trejo for finding carpenters and laborers, which have been in short supply, in Ojinaga, and for overseeing the work.

I looked at Clay. "It sounds like Trejo was around all the time, so he and my mother would have seen a lot of each other. She mentions how often the construction crew came into the trading post." I turned over several pages of the notebook. "Apparently the film crew arrived next, in mid-May, along with staff and French again. That's when she wrote this."

> Justice is gone from me, back into the black spirits that rob him of all joy and peace of mind. He has given up on doctors. He has gone to stay at Mother and Dad's cabin at the ranch. He says being alone is the only thing that seems to help. But that doesn't help me. I wish I could have back for just one hour the man that I married. I'm glad the movie people are here. It takes my mind off Justice. The trading post has been so busy, I've hired Deida Luna to help wait on customers.

"The next entries are later, after the actors had arrived."

> The crew and some of the actors have made the trading post their hangout. I'm staying open until ten each night. They come in after dinner, to play poker and drink Carta Blanca.

"She had opinions on all of them, too," I told Clay. "Just listen."

> Jon French is amazingly patient with the crew and the actors. He works longer and harder than anyone.

"Listen to what she wrote about Rosalinda Pray."

> Behind all the spoiled brat temper tantrums and flaunting of her sexuality, I think she is as lonely as I am.

"This is her first personal comment about Trejo."

> I think people who have seen much suffering, as Jacinto did during the revolution, either become hardened and callous, or else understanding and compassionate, like him.

"It's only much later, when the movie is nearly finished, that she writes about her feelings for him."

> I didn't realize how long I'd been unhappy, my unspoken fears unrelieved by silent tears at night. Jacinto has brought laughter and joy back into my life. It's been so long since I felt there was someone I could rely on. And the happiness. It's wonderful to have someone to talk to. I love him for loving me.

"There's only one more mention of Trejo before his murder."

> The filming will be over in less than a week and the stars and crew will leave the next morning after the final scene is shot. Jacinto is very preoccupied. I asked him if he was worried about me, about leaving, but he said no. I asked him, "What then?" He was very quiet for a while, then he said, "Moxicuani always smiles." I recognized the *dicho,* but I didn't know why he used it. I asked him what he meant, but he just shook his head.

"Who's this Moxicuani?" Clay asked.

"The devil," I said, "but not the Anglo version. Moxicuani is a horseman. He's always pictured wearing a sombrero and gold spurs." I turned over the pages of the journal to the entry dated July fifteenth. "This is my mother's last entry."

> Jacinto is dead. Murdered. I can't bear it, the loss of his kindness and strength. The last time I saw him was the day they shot the fiesta scene. He told me he was going to meet with someone afterward. I never saw him again. The funeral was in his home village, Cuchillo Parado. Mr. French and the crew chief went to represent the movie company. I didn't go. People would have thought it odd. My loving him was no crime, but people would talk. How I wish that I could have taken flowers to put on his grave.

"That's the final entry," I said, closing the journal.

Clay got up and went to the counter. I heard him rummaging in shelves, running water, then the microwave. In five minutes he was back with a cup of hot spiced tea.

I took it gratefully, cupping my hands around its warmth

because I felt so cold. "Our lives, my parents' and mine, were a lie."

Clay sat down again, saying mildly, "You're assuming your mother slept with this man. But you don't know that. There are all kinds of love."

"It still hurts to know how unhappy she was. She would have been thirty that summer. Trejo must have been at least twenty years older."

"About the age I am now, probably," Clay said.

"You know, even now, whenever I visit Dad, or even telephone, I always pray that I'm going to catch him on a good day. After my mother died, when he was so bad, I was afraid every time I called home that there'd be no answer because he'd killed himself. Imagine how she felt all those years. But for me, she was always cheerful. I don't remember her ever using the word 'depression.' When Dad would vanish for days into his study, she'd say that he needed privacy. When he took to going off for days and weeks alone, she'd say he was on a camping trip. I thought my family was the norm, like most kids, I guess. I never doubted that my father loved me, but my mother raised me by herself, really."

"Regardless of Trejo," Clay said, "if she'd wanted to leave, she could have taken you and gone to live at her parents' ranch."

"Maybe she stayed because she thought she didn't have any choice. Maybe she stayed because of me." I felt slightly queasy.

"There are always choices," Clay said firmly. "Your mother made hers. I think second-guessing her now would be unfair to her."

That's what I love about my husband. When I most need him, he's always there. He doesn't try to protect me from reality, but he offers comfort when I need it. I put aside the journal, finished my tea, feeling safe in Clay's companionship and counting myself very lucky.

Clay touched my shoulder lightly. "I'm going to take a shower, then we'll talk some more."

I nodded absently and finished the tea. I was washing the cup when I saw Nellie come around the corner to the back door. He had raised his hand to knock when I opened it.

"Are you a mind reader, or was that luck?" he said, smiling.

"A view from the rear window," I said, inviting him in.

"I'm delivering a message. Mr. Anthony would like you and your husband to come for dinner, say around seven-thirty. It's entirely casual. He emphasized that you were to come as you are."

I said we would be delighted, and halfway meant it. It would give me something else to think about other than my mother's journal. The telephone rang, and Nellie said he would see us later. I answered on the second ring. A small boy was saying something about a puppy. I managed to get the child's name. His family lived in Polvo. I went to interrupt Clay's shower to tell him he was needed.

Clay was still gone when Scott and Chris finished their last taping session at seven. At seven-twenty he came in.

"You just have time to wash your hands. We're going out to dinner."

FOURTEEN

Dane Anthony sat in a leather chair, looking very western in the clothes I had given him from my stock, his feet resting comfortably on the ottoman. Clay and I were on the couch. Chris occupied a second armchair, and Jenna and Scott sat on barstools. Behind the bar Nellie mixed drinks. From the CD player on the built-in sideboard Andrea Bocelli serenaded us. The round coffee table held platters of cheese, sesame seed crackers, vegetable spread, and smoked turkey sandwiches.

"I raided Scott's larder," Dane said. "Help yourselves. Where's Jeremy?"

"In the middle of making some prints of the horse rescue," Scott said. "That's all he and Chris can talk about. I think, Clay, they'd rather be working on that video."

Dane wanted to hear about the rescue, and Clay gave him a condensed version as Nellie handed out margaritas in frosted glasses.

"The drink was invented by a restaurateur in Juarez, you

know." Dane sipped his with evident pleasure. "Named for his wife."

The actor had the necessary qualities of a good host—the ability to put his guests at ease and to manage the conversation so as to include everyone. He told several well-chosen stories about the filming of *Panchito* that had us laughing. Over a second round of drinks he drew Chris out about his plans for the horse video, questioned Scott about his previous projects, and managed to get the quiet Jenna to talk about what she called "a spooky experience" on the drive back from Presidio.

"Scott was driving. I was looking out the window at the river. I saw something move in the trees. It was huge, and it had this brown stuff hanging all over it. Then it vanished. It was creepy."

"She yelled for me to look," Scott said. "At first I didn't see anything, then it moved again. I admit, it spooked me for a second. I slowed down, and whoever it was ran for cover. Too bad I didn't have one of the video cameras. I missed my chance to catch the giant Fungus Monster of the Rio Grande."

The others laughed. Clay caught my eye and grinned.

"Scott thinks it was a hunter. I think it was one of those weird survivalists playing a war game," Jenna said.

"What you saw," Clay said, "was member of the Texas National Guard wearing a ghillie suit. A serious sort of camouflage that covers even the head."

"We call them 'river watchers,' " I said. "They're patrolling, trying to identify the most popular crossings for drug smuggling."

"The soldier probably heard you coming and was trying to get your license plate number," Clay said. "We assume they keep tabs on vehicles, too."

"Speaking of vehicles," Scott said, "I've noticed most people around here drive General Motors cars and trucks. Why is that?"

"That's what the local dealership in Marfa sells," Clay said.

"If you drive something else and you want warranty work, it's a heck of a drive. 'Course, Texana loves her Ford."

"That's because Polvo has a good shade tree mechanic," I said.

That turned the talk to local subjects: the Marfa lights, Fort Leaton, the devil's cave outside Ojinaga.

"No Man's Land," Dane said. "Is the island still there? Or has the river claimed it?"

"Still there," I said.

"Jon French decided to use it for the site where Pancho Villa leaves Ernestine Moore after the ransom has been paid," Dane said. "The script called for the scene to take place in Mexico, but Jon thought No Man's Land more picturesque and romantic. He was intrigued by its lack of any kind of jurisdictional status." He turned to Scott. "You should include it in the video. You could juxtapose Rosalinda there talking about it and show the film clip of her standing there alone as Villa rides toward Mexico and her husband rides across from the other side. When is Rosy coming back, by the way?"

"Tomorrow," Scott said. "We'll be videotaping the village site with her."

With the mention of No Man's Land, a thought had hit me hard. I was oblivious to the remainder of the conversation and grateful when Nellie served coffee and, after a decent interval, the party broke up.

"You got very quiet," Clay said as we stepped over the concrete parking barriers that separated the RV lot from the trading post parking. "Are you okay?"

"I was thinking about Jacinto Trejo's murder. You heard what Tom Putnam said at the party. It wasn't robbery. No one had any explanation for it. And it happened at a place that every local knew about, a perfect place for a murder. It doesn't belong to the United States. It doesn't belong to Mexico. That meant neither side would spend much time trying to solve the crime. The law just went through the motions. The way Hap tells it, the biggest worry was who would pay for the funeral. A local would have appreciated all that."

"That makes sense."

We had reached the back door. I put my hand on Clay's arm to stop him for a moment. "What if my father found out about Mother and Trejo? What if he killed Trejo?"

FIFTEEN

In all the intervening years since my mother's death, I had avoided thinking of her. I coped with her death by denying her life, by not bringing it too close to me, because it was painful. She was gone before I had time to know her as a person rather than merely as my mother, before I could ask her the hundreds of questions that I have thought of since her death.

Her journal had thrust her life back into mine, forcing me to consider what happened forty years ago.

I got out of bed as quietly as I could and closed the bedroom door behind me. I turned on the lamp by the couch, got the flashlight, and walked through to the front to get one of the copies of *Panchito* from the video rentals.

Like most of Polvo, my parents and I had attended the premiere at the Palace Theater in Marfa, but what I remembered of the movie came from watching it once on television when I was in college.

I didn't care about seeing it all the way through again. I

watched the opening credits: Garner Studio presents a Three Minds Production; Producer-Director Jon French; Associate Producer Dane Anthony.

The movie opens with Villa leading his men on a raid against a hacienda. I fast-forwarded the video until the last scene. No Man's Land looks larger on film than it does in reality, a trick of perspective. Rainfall in 1961 must have been above normal: the river was running high enough to reach the horses' shoulders as you see Villa and his captive riding across from Mexico for the exchange. As Villa, Dane Anthony wore the costume from the movie poster illustration: a huge sombrero, a matching black jacket, tight-fitting Mexican trousers with silver buttons down the sides, and spurs on his boots. Rosalinda Pray, playing Ernestine Moore, had been costumed in a dark green fitted jacket that is dusty from the ride, and her long skirts are damp from the river crossing. A sombrero shades her fair skin from the desert sun.

But it was the island itself that interested me, as if I could read there the story of murder among the waving green plants and the twisted roots of the solitary salt cedar. I muted the sound and hardly noticed the silent stars mouthing their lines. I watched the background. But the sandy little island told me nothing.

The closing shot is of the tall elegant figure of Ernestine Moore, the sombrero she has worn held in her hands, standing in the middle of the island watching as Villa rides away in one direction and her husband rides in from the other.

I rewound the tape, replaced it on the rental shelf, and went back to bed.

SIXTEEN

You should go see your father."

"And say what? 'Did you know your wife loved another man? Did you kill him?' "

Clay put down his fork and got up from the breakfast table. "You're letting this business of the journal change the way you feel about your father. Before you judge him, you should talk to him."

"I know. But I'm scared. I don't want to believe it's possible that my father did such a thing. But I have to consider it."

What I remembered most about the ceaseless anxiety that smothered the joy out of my father's life were the outbursts of ungoverned anger at the smallest things: the pickup that wouldn't start, a key breaking off in a lock, a sheet of tin blowing off the trading post roof. And I remembered my mother's constant efforts to shield him from any worry or trouble, however small. If my father had treated the trials of daily life as tribulations, how would he have reacted to betrayal? And why had I used that word? Because I thought it myself? If my father had been diagnosed with a physical illness, would my mother have felt as lost and alone? As needy? I wished that I had never found the journal.

Lost in my own misery, I barely reacted when Clay leaned over, rested his hand on my shoulder, and kissed the top of my head. He collected his jacket and his keys and went to the back door. "I'll be at the Cross T Ranch most of the day."

I sat there, the food on my plate uneaten. The ceiling light cast a bright glow over the table, while outside the sunrise had barely lightened the night.

I put on a jacket and went out. It was miserably cold. The lack of humidity plunges the temperature at night, then sends the thermometer soaring with full sunlight. It is freeze or roast in the desert.

I turned the corner of the trading post, crossed the parking lot and the road, and descended to the riverbank. The bank runs uneven and rugged. The mesquite grows deep and thick, and the whispery clump grass juts up from pockets of sandy soil trapped by the rocks streaked with brown and gray.

I walked, anxiety dropping away as I went. The air smelled of creosote and the river. I filled my lungs and emptied my mind. I wasn't conscious of having made a decision, but when I was done, I went to see Dane Anthony.

Nellie answered my knock. "Mr. Anthony just finished breakfast." Behind him, Dane called, "Come in, come in. Company is always welcome."

His wheelchair was by the window that overlooked the hills behind the trading post. An IV bag attached to a portable metal frame dangled above his head, the drip tube running into the needle in his arm.

"Don't be alarmed," he said, gesturing with his free arm at the setup. "Chelation therapy. It puts vitamins and minerals directly into the bloodstream. Nellie hooks me up. Makes me feel much stronger. It's not only for those of us with health problems. Start now and it will keep you healthy."

"Where do you get this supplement?" I asked.

"From a homeopathic doctor back home. When my supply went up in smoke with the RV, I thought I'd have to do without. But Nellie located a source in town the day he went with poor Gwen to the hospital. Have Nellie give you the name."

Nellie brought me a cup of coffee, then left us, saying he'd be making the beds if he was needed.

"I watched *Panchito* last night on videotape. The last part, on the island, especially interests me."

Dane put down his coffee cup. "I played some of my finest scenes on that little sandbar. Films aren't shot in the order of the story line, you know. That scene was one of the first we did. There were takes and retakes. Three days of work to get five minutes of film time. The weather was so hot the pancake makeup rolled off our faces with the sweat, so every few minutes the makeup artists would have to repair the damage. The highlight of the day was getting into the shade of the tent and having a cold Bloody Mary with lunch."

"It must have been a tight squeeze, getting everyone onto that small place," I said.

"You're so right, my dear. Jon kept an open set. Anyone could come and go. On any given day we usually had reporters and lots of local people to watch the filming. But not for the island. It was just the camera crew, Jon's assistants, and the makeup people. He even had the caterers pack the lunches. We served ourselves."

"It must have been a shock all those weeks later when Jacinto Trejo's body turned up there."

"Tragic. It was a great distress to all of us when he was killed. I didn't know him well, mind you. There wasn't much time for socializing. I think Jon was devastated by his murder. After all, the man wouldn't have been there if Jon hadn't hired him."

"What was the talk," I asked, "about why he might have been killed?"

"There wasn't much."

"But surely—"

"By that time we were only days away from winding up the filming. Everyone was looking forward to going home and relaxing for a while after the intensity of all those weeks. I seem to recall that the local authorities had some idea about smuggling."

"Do you think his death was in any way connected to the movie?"

"I can't imagine what connection there could have been. He wasn't one of us. It was much more likely to have been a local affair, surely?"

"Did the sheriff question anyone in particular?"

"Someone talked to the cast and crew as a group. Wanting to know when we'd seen him last. That sort of thing," Dane said. "It was brief and very general. Sort of, 'if anybody knows anything, get in touch.' "

I stayed twenty more minutes as he talked about the film, but nothing he told me shed any light on the murder of the *villista.* To Dane Anthony, the man had been merely one among many, like camera and makeup crew, who had worked in the background.

Clay was right. I needed to see my father. But not today. This day would be full. In a couple of hours Rosalinda Pray would be here, and I had promised to conduct the crew to the site of the movie village.

SEVENTEEN

Word passes, and swiftly. Everyone seemed to know that Rosalinda Pray would be making an appearance. By ten most of Polvo was in the trading post parking lot in anticipation of her arrival. Scott and Chris had wrapped up the second videotaping session of the day and were loading equipment in the Range Rover for the drive to the old location site. I was taking advantage of the lull to open briefly for business.

I had customers lined up at the register when I heard a familiar sound. I followed the wheeze and saw the man with the oxygen tank leaning against the end of the counter, wide arms folded across his chest. He wore a brown corduroy jacket with navy slacks and a blue shirt. His bolo tie had a turquoise clasp. His lank hair had been combed over, emphasizing the baldness it was intended to hide.

I was ringing up the sale of a pair of jeans, two shirts, and a bottle of mange medicine when he was joined by two people I knew slightly, one of whom had been talking with him the night of the party at Tia's Cafe. Bill Desto was the reporter for the *International*, Presidio's weekly. I thought the second man's name was Mott. He wrote for the Alpine newspaper, meaning Rosalinda's fame had spread to the next county. Her publicist at work? But who did the wheezing man work for?

At ten-forty everyone but the trio of reporters had moved outside to see Rosalinda Pray arrive. I was ready to close out the register when Dennis Bustamante strolled in to pay for gas, his boyish face as friendly as a puppy's. Dennis was a friend, a lifetime local, and a good lawman. The deputy sheriff worked out of Presidio and covered the lower half of the county.

"You here for crowd control?" I asked as Dennis handed me a fifty for his thirty-eight dollars' worth of gas.

"Sort of. Things are quiet in south Presidio County."

"Our visitors don't think so."

"Yeah, I heard about the fire."

"You haven't heard about the monster our visitors saw."

"You mean we've got a Big Foot?" he said, grinning.

I told him about Scott and Jenna seeing the soldier, but Dennis didn't laugh as I had expected him to. "I don't know what they saw, but it wasn't a soldier. They've been pulled out."

"Since when?"

"About ten days ago."

"So what did they see?"

"A poacher maybe. I'll check with the commander and see if his bunch is missing any camouflage." Dennis folded his money and put it in his billfold. "Give me a call if any of you spot this guy again."

Dennis left. I took the cash out of the register and locked it away. Mott was checking his watch. "She should be here any minute."

"We've got time. Pray's always late," the wheezy man said, coming up to the register to pay for a candy bar.

I made change out of my pocket. "Sounds like you know her well."

"I know her reputation." He extended his hand. Mine came away slightly moist. "Luther Carmondy."

"Luther's writing for *Texas Monthly,*" Bill Desto said, awe in his voice.

"We're moving in high cotton," Mott said.

"I don't work for the magazine," Carmondy explained. "I'm freelance. They asked me to do a piece on the video. I was a movie critic for the *San Antonio Telegram* when *Panchito* was made."

Mott smiled slightly. "What's your take on this curse business?"

"The curse on *Panchito* was bad directing, bad script, and mediocre acting," Carmondy said.

"There were two deaths, an accident and a murder," Mott said.

Desto said, "Who was murdered?"

"A Mexican national named Trejo. He was some kind of consultant," Mott said. "They found his body four days before the movie company wrapped the film."

"How did you know that?" Desto asked.

"I checked the back issues." Desto reddened.

Carmondy was about to speak when Nellie pushed Dane Anthony into the room. "Gentlemen, nice to see you again. I'm at your service for interviews," the actor said.

"Let's talk," Carmondy said, pulling his portable oxygen tank along as he aimed for the table. I joined everyone else on the porch.

True to Carmondy's prediction, Rosalinda Pray did not show up until nearly noon, by which time not a few of the locals had given up and gone home, though the reporters and Carmondy stayed.

The actress's cowboy driver rolled the car up to the steps and got out to open the door for her. Scott was right there waiting, but instead of offering her cheek for the ritual kiss, she handed him a long cardboard cylinder. If she was disappointed by the small number of people watching her entrance, she didn't show it. She marched up the steps smiling, Pippa the dog tucked under one arm. As always, Chris was there with the video camera.

She walked straight into the trading post without a backward glance at those locals who had waited for so long. She yanked off her sunglasses and looked over at Dane's chair pulled up to the table where the reporters sat. "Dane, did you start the interviews without me?"

"Just warming them up, Rosy."

She marched in their direction while telling Scott the cylinder was for me.

He handed it over. Carmondy and the two reporters rose as the actress joined them. Chris stopped taping, and Jeremy removed the roll of film he'd shot. Dane rolled toward the photographer and spoke briefly with him, then rejoined the others.

I opened the cardboard tube and unrolled an autographed movie poster: Dane Anthony as Pancho Villa in sombrero, bandaliers, and spurs, sitting on a black horse with Rosalinda Pray, as Ernestine Moore, standing beside the horse looking up at him. I took it to the back and put it on the table, then sat down to wait until the interviews were over and Scott was ready to go. There was no track to the village site since it was seldom that anyone went there, so I had agreed to show Scott the way.

An hour and a half later the reporters left. Scott escorted the actress and her dog to the Range Rover, but when she saw me getting into my pickup, she insisted on riding with me.

"Unless you want Pippa to stay in the pickup the whole time, you might want to leave her here."

"Why?"

"Rattlesnakes."

She handed me the dog. I held her away from me, and the pee splashed on the ground. I carried the nervous animal to the kennel and shut her safely inside.

"Thanks for the poster," I said, slipping back behind the wheel.

"I brought it to give my hosts, but you saved Pippa," she said, fastening her seatbelt.

We drove up the low hill behind Clay's office and out across the desert scrub. The village site was located at nearly dead center of my 640 acres. As the pickup bumped over the ground, birds took flight out of the scrub. A flash of white caught my eye. I watched as the harrier skimmed along the ground. In the time it took me to blink the hawk dropped like a thunderbolt, struck with its talons, and rose with a black-throated sparrow in its grasp. Beside me, Rosalinda Pray frowned down at a chipped red fingernail on her left hand, oblivious to life and death.

"Your idea about publicity seems to be working," I said. "You got *Texas Monthly* interested."

"Carmondy? That old fart. He's nothing. But before this is over, we'll get national press."

After that she sat back and watched the scenery, not speaking again until we drove within sight of the village.

"I expected it to be a ruin," Rosalinda said in an astonished voice. "It looks just the same as when we filmed. You know Jon went to all this trouble for authenticity."

After the *adoberos* had raised the walls, paint crews had slapped on the bright hues of red, yellow, turquoise, and green, colors that give life to the most humble homes in Mexico. The buildings had been hurriedly built, not intended to last, but though the paint had faded, the walls remained intact, thanks to our scant rainfall and dry climate. Looking at them in the bright sunlight, I half-expected people to come out and welcome us as we parked and got out.

While Scott and Chris positioned the camera on a tripod and set up the portable generator, I walked around. It had been a long time since I'd visited the site. Until we had outgrown such play, Pete Rosales, his sister Chata, my best friend Maria, and I had used the adobes as our private place, pretending to be bandits hiding from the Texas Rangers. We had kept a stash of chocolates and cigarettes and Cokes and spent hours enjoying our contraband.

While Scott gave brief directions to Rosalinda Pray and Chris tested her voice level, I circled the adobes. One wall had bowed out on the adobe that had been our childhood hiding place. I stepped into the empty doorway. The single room beyond was in shadow, but in one corner something lay bunched, a huddled shape that might have been a person. The dirt floor was littered with bits of small animal bones and droppings that had been crushed where someone had walked repeatedly between the door and the corner. Eight steps and I was standing over the pile of rags in the corner.

The light from the door was enough for me to identify what I was looking at. I picked it up, shaking it to make sure that no snake was hibernating in or under it, and carried it outside.

What I had found was a hooded jacket and pants in brown and tan hunter's camouflage with burlap strips about an inch wide attached all over with big, crude stitches.

EIGHTEEN

What *have* you got?" Rosalinda asked.

I'd been so engrossed in my find that I hadn't heard anyone approach. Not only the actress, but Chris, Jeremy, Scott, and Jenna stood staring at the garments in my hands in fascination.

"Hey, it's what you said the man by the river wore, isn't it?" Chris said, looking at Jenna and Scott.

"What's a ghillie suit doing up here?" Scott asked. "Does the Texas National Guard use this place for maneuvers?"

"This suit isn't Guard issue," I said.

"How do you know that?" Jenna asked.

"See the red lettering on some of the strips?" I said.

"Does it say something?" Rosalinda asked.

"It would read "Whole Growth" if you fit it together. These strips were cut from burlap bags that hold a special blend of cattle feed. I sell it at the trading post."

"So," Scott said, "you think it *was* a hunter we saw?"

"It's possible," I said, folding the garments. "A lot of hunting goes on along the river."

"Are you taking it?" Jenna asked.

"I'll show it to the game warden," I said. "You're quite sure the person you saw didn't have a rifle?"

"If he had one," Scott said, "we didn't see it." Jenna nodded in agreement.

"I'll put this in the pickup," I said, moving away. The crew went back to work.

I placed the ghillie suit behind the seat. Even supposing there had been rifle, whoever had worn the garment had been out at the wrong time of day for a hunter. Most game is nocturnal. Prime hunting time is just after dawn or at dusk, not mid-afternoon. A casual hunter might take potshots at anything at any time of day, but not someone so serious as to go to the trouble of wearing camouflage. The jacket and pants belonged to no hunter. I would show them to Dennis.

The taping took two hours, at the end of which Chris turned the camera slowly away from Rosalinda to sweep the hills slipping down to the river, the ridges below studded with the whipped branches of ocotillo, sotol, and lechuguilla.

I had thought Rosalinda might make the return trip with the others, but as Chris loaded his equipment she joined me in the pickup. Scott waved a hand, signaling he was ready to leave, and I started the motor.

"I didn't realize how much it would warm up," Rosalinda said, rolling up the long sleeves of her shirt and wiping the perspiration from her brow with a tissue.

"There's bottled water in the container behind the seat," I said.

"Do you want one?" She leaned around between the seats. I shook my head, and she got one for herself, drank deeply, recapped the bottle, and set it in the holder below the dash.

"How long have you been married?" she said.

"Nineteen years."

"That's a long time to be married to the same person. Clay, isn't that his name? Is he your first husband?"

"He's the only one I count, I was married briefly right after college."

"I've given up on husbands," Rosalinda said. "Now I just have friends."

"That puts you in charge, I guess. There's nothing wrong with that."

"You're saying that for my sake, but you don't really believe it," Rosalinda said firmly.

"I wouldn't have the stamina for it, that's all," I said. "I think if anything happened to Clay, I'd live alone."

"I hate being alone," Rosalinda said. She gave a hard laugh with no humor in it. "Of course, after a certain age it can be as hard to find companionship as film parts, but take it from me, when it comes to companionship, money is the best plastic surgeon."

I laughed. "I'll keep it in mind if I ever get any. Money, I mean."

Rosy kept quiet for the rest of the ride. As we reached the downslope behind the trading post I saw a kid, a strange vehicle, and a man I didn't recognize in the RV lot. The man seemed to be examining the debris around Dane's burned-out motor home. I parked the pickup by the back door. Scott drove by, going around to the front to unload the equipment. Rosalinda made no move to get out.

"What I said yesterday, about your mother and Jacinto," she said. "I wish that just once in my life a man had looked at me the way he looked at her. As if the whole world and all he had ever wanted was in her face. She was loved. Not all of us can say that."

She opened the door, stepped out, and slammed it behind her. Jimmy Ramos came around the corner of the trading post. The twelve-year-old was wearing a yellow knit shirt with the tail out, jeans so blue they had to be new, and badly scuffed white tennis shoes.

"*Hola,* Jimmy," I said, getting out of the pickup. "Shouldn't you be on the school bus about now?"

"Dane said if I came by at two he'd show me the gunbelt and hat he wore when he was Pancho Villa. He let me try them on. Then the guy who's taking pictures of that burned trailer showed up, and Dane said I better go. So I just hung out. What time is it?" he asked anxiously.

I checked my watch. "Ten after five."

"I gotta go," Jimmy shouted as he darted around the corner the way he'd come.

"What's he in such a hurry for?" Rosalinda asked.

"He wants to get to the school bus when the other kids are dropped off so he can walk home with them. That way his mother won't know he cut school."

"I sympathize with the kid," Rosalinda said. "I hated school myself."

There was a frantic barking from the kennels. I went to release Pippa and take her back to Rosalinda. This time the dog peed before I picked her up.

"Make yourself at home inside," I told her. "I'll be in as soon as I check with Scott." I walked around the corner to see what was going on in the RV lot. Scott stood talking to a serious-looking man in shirt, slacks, windbreaker, and a pair of heavy-duty shoes. He motioned me over, and I joined then.

"Lee Brown," the man said, shaking my hand. "I'm with the State Fire Marshal's Office. The insurance company asked us to look into this. Judging by the debris field, you folks were lucky only two people were hurt. I was telling Mr. Regan here that until I have the ash samples analyzed I can't say if gasoline or some other combustible was used. I can tell you the fire didn't start in the engine. The question is, where did it start, and how?"

"Are you saying it was arson?"

"Like I told Mr. Anthony, I can't find any accidental cause. I understand there were a lot of people around shortly before

Mr. Anthony spotted the smoke. Could be someone used a simple paper fuse, like a rolled-up newspaper with one end touching something like a couch or a curtain." He shifted his weight from one foot to another. "The easiest is a lit cigarette closed in a book of matches. Toss it in and wait." He jerked his thumb in the direction of what was left of the RV. "Almost everything in these things is made of petroleum-based synthetics. The subfloors and walls are pressed board or particle board to lighten the vehicle's weight. Both highly flammable. With the air from the open windows to feed the fire, you'd have full flame in a very short time. If those gas canisters hadn't exploded, the fire would have consumed the motor home in maybe twenty minutes."

I glanced at Scott, trying to read his face, but his expression was as neutral as Switzerland. Had he told Lee Brown about the warning note? I said nothing. Let the investigation take its course. We didn't know whether the fire and the note were connected. Nothing else had happened since.

I left the two still talking and went to get the ghillie suit out of the pickup in case the owner came looking for it at the adobe and followed the tire tracks back here. I didn't want it disappearing before I could show it to Dennis.

I had forgotten all about Rosalinda Pray, who stood at the back door looking exasperated.

"Where is everyone?" she said impatiently. "If Scott is quite through with me, I'd like to leave."

I explained why Scott was delayed, thinking of her poor driver, waiting out front all afternoon.

Pippa squirmed in her arms. "I'll have to wait until the investigator is gone. He'll want an autograph, and I simply do not feel like being my public self." She went inside.

I retrieved the ghillie suit, carried it in, and draped it over one of the dining chairs.

Rosalinda marched through our living quarters to the front. I could hear her high voice telling Scott how she thought the morning's taping should be edited. He made a much softer answer that I couldn't make out. In a few minutes Rosalinda came back and sat down on the couch.

"Chris was telling me about rescuing the horses. Tell me about this man Arias who's taking care of them."

"My husband says every animal has a distinct personality. Cinco appreciates that in his horses and works with each one as an individual. He doesn't just heal them physically. He heals them emotionally by letting them know they are loved. He restores their faith in humans. When the horse is ready, he finds it a home. He makes sure the new owners understand the commitment of time and love that caring for an animal requires. He keeps track of every horse he places. If an owner can't cope, or moves, or dies, Cinco takes the animal back. He does what he does out of love. That's why he prefers to work alone. That way he has what you might call total 'quality control.' "

"I must meet this Mr. Arias," Rosalinda Pray said. "I'm very active in animal rights. I can promise him all kinds of support for his horse hospital. We could generate enough in donations so he could employ help. Think of the number of animals he could save then." She raised her voice. "Chris, come in here." She turned her attention back to me, her eyes alight with excitement. When Chris came in, she said, "I'm going to visit Mr. Arias. Chris, you're going to come with us and tape the visit. I'll arrange things with Scott. I think I'd be the perfect spokesperson for the . . . what does he call his place?"

"His ranch is the Two Bar," I said.

"He doesn't have a name for the horse rehab," Chris said. "It's more a vocation with him. Not a business."

"Then you're in charge of coming up with one," Rosalinda said. "This will be great publicity."

I thought of whether or not Cinco, being a private person, would want such publicity. But he could speak for himself.

Scott came looking for his video star. The three went into the front. I got a glass, dropped in an ice cube, poured myself a whiskey, and put my feet up. I wanted five minutes in which I didn't have to talk, think, or do anything.

I didn't get my wish. Someone knocked at the back door. Nellie stood there loaded down with grocery bags.

"Mr. Anthony sent me to Presidio for fresh vegetables and meat. I seem to have bought more than the RV's refrigerator will hold," he said.

"You've come to the right place. I've got a walk-in cooler."

After he left, I fell asleep on the couch. When I woke, I heard the shower running. Clay was home. Outside the light was going. From somewhere hard to pinpoint, the staccato barking of a coyote began, then the long howl, pitched like a siren, and finally the mixed-note yipping that makes the lone animal seem like many. The coyotes outnumber us here in the borderland. Polveños keep their small dogs locked up at night so the coyotes won't get them. When I was eight my new puppy was killed by a coyote that dug under the fence of the dog run. The next morning my father had tracked the coyote and killed it.

I sat up. Soon, very soon, I would have to confront my fears and go and see my father.

NINETEEN

I took the first turn past the Border Patrol checkpoint on Highway 67 between Marfa and Presidio, putting the morning sun behind me. I had left home while Clay was still in the shower. The track was so rough that I wondered how long it had been since my father had it graded. But then, as he never went anywhere and seldom had visitors, the condition of the three-mile track was of little concern to him.

The ranch had belonged to my maternal grandparents, who died in an automobile accident and left it divided between my mother and her brother. After my mother's death, Dad had sold all but three thousand acres and the easement.

The solitude of the place had somehow saved him when medicine and doctors could not. His peace of mind was hard-won and precarious, but real. He spent his days mending fence, tending cattle, and maintaining the well and the pipeline that fed the house and the water troughs in the five pastures. For company he had half a dozen longhorn cows so old they were almost toothless, a dog named Woo Hoo, a cat named Willie, and, temporarily, our bobcat.

No livestock, pet, or person was in sight when I pulled up the last hill and drove down into the depression where the white frame house sits, almost as if it had been built for the purpose of protecting my father from the world with which he coped so poorly.

I parked in front of the house and got out. The slam of the pickup door echoed against both hills.

"Over here." My father's voice came from behind the barn. I crossed the dry coarse grass that lay between house and outbuilding, and on around to the back of the barn.

My father stood at the base of the utility pole. At his feet sat a brown and white mutt with floppy ears and a gray, short-haired cat. Atop the pole was a much bigger cat, with black tipped ears, a short tail, and large paws that clung tightly to her perch.

"What's Phobe doing up there?"

"I think she took umbrage at something Woo Hoo did."

"In that case, how come it isn't the dog on top of the pole?" I said, and got a tenuous smile from my father.

Looking at him was like looking in a mirror and seeing my own face twenty years hence. There's no mistaking the likeness. He is pure Italian, the image of his grandfather Franco. The hawkish Neopolitan nose is the first giveaway. His eyebrows are sharply etched below a broad forehead. His brown eyes are deep-set and reflect his moods as much as the full-lipped mouth that turns down in sorrow more often than it curls up in laughter. But it is the thin frame and taut skin that are the hallmarks of the emotional stress that consumes so much of his energy.

"Do you have a ladder?" I asked.

"I was about to fetch it." He disappeared around the barn and came back with the ladder he used for roof repairs.

"Shall I, or do you think she'd prefer you?" he asked as he propped it against the pole.

"I'll go." He held the bottom of the ladder. I climbed, talking to Phobe as I went. When I got close enough to reach her, I stroked her head. Slowly and carefully, I got her by the scruff of the neck with one hand and lifted, no easy task with a twenty-pound bobcat. She snarled and spit, but she didn't scratch. I transferred my hold to my other hand, putting it under her chest and holding her half over my shoulder. With only one hand to hold the ladder, the climb down was slow. As soon as my feet touched the ground, I released her. Willie the cat turned slowly and walked away. Phobe turned on Woo Hoo, narrowed her eyes, and spit. The mutt whimpered and lay flat, head between his paws, groveling. She grabbed an ear, and they went round and round, but this time it was play, not fighting, because Woo Hoo's fluffy tail wagged furiously. From the security of six feet away, Willie maintained a dignified demeanor and observed.

"What caused all this?" I asked as my father lowered the ladder.

"I found a coyote pup sitting by its dead mother. Between bottles it likes to suck on Phobe's fur like a pacifier. Woo Hoo keeps picking the pup up and carrying it off. I don't know if he's jealous of Phobe or trying to mother the pup himself. Come see it. I'll put the ladder up later."

We went in the back door, the cats and dog coming after us. A fat-bellied coyote pup slept in a basket by the gas heater in the kitchen. Phobe went over, sniffed at his head, then curled beside the basket protectively.

I touched the pup's fuzzy fur. "What's his name?"

"It's too early to say. Depends on what he's like when I get to know him better."

"Would you like Clay to have a look at him?"

Dad nodded. "That would be good. Sit down and I'll fix us some coffee."

I sat at the kitchen table watching him. He moved with economy, saving energy with the same frugality by which he reserved his fragile emotions. Woo Hoo followed us as we took our cups out to the porch. It looked out over the ten fruit trees planted by my father as one of his first projects after he had moved here permanently. We sat in silence, our own and nature's. The hills cupped around the house and yard, making the space seem like an island floating beneath the broad sky. My father spent long hours on this porch. I had once arrived after dark and found him there, in a sleeping bag, the dog and cat curled up alongside.

"I've had a good few weeks," he said. An oblique reference to his state of mind. He generally spoke with this kind of quiet precision, like someone who had mastered stammering, but only with great care. "How about you?"

I looked at my father's gaunt face, which wore calm like an inflexible mask that would shatter if struck. "I've been okay," I said.

"You look like you're worried about something."

"I've got some people staying at the RV park," I said.

"You talking about the ones making some television show about that Pancho Villa movie?" Woo Hoo had settled at his feet, and he was rubbing the dog with his foot.

"How'd you hear about it?"

"The well man told me when he came out to replace the pump. Cost me nine hundred dollars. When I first moved out here, you could nearly drill a well for that."

I shifted in my chair. My father never left home but always knew what was going on. What about forty years ago? Had he known then?

"I'll be glad when they're gone," I said. "It's tiresome having people always around."

"You're telling me?"

I laughed, glad that he could make a joke about his need for solitude.

"What was it like when the movie people were here back in sixty-one?" I asked, skirting the real question I could never ask, yet half fearful of what his reaction might be to even an innocuous reference to those days.

"I only stayed around long enough to make sure they gave

your mother and me a fair deal for the use of the land, then I came out to your granddad's guest house. Your mother probably enjoyed the excitement. Made a nice change for her."

"Did she say so?"

"She didn't talk about it much." He put his cup down on the floor of the porch, clasped his hands together, and began to rotate one thumb around the other in tight little circles. It was a sign of tension. Usually when he did this, it meant the visit had gone on long enough and it was time for me to go. Did it mean that now, or did the tension stem from some remembered anxiety relating to the subject of my mother? I kept still and quiet.

"Sometimes," he said pensively, "I forget how old I am. Then I look in the mirror. I don't feel so much different than I did at thirty. I don't mean physically. I mean in my mind and my heart."

"I understand, Dad. I'm getting older, too."

Willie the cat jumped into my lap, circled twice, then settled down. I rubbed his head behind the ears, and he purred.

"Your mother always kept me up on the news. Who came in to the trading post, who was engaged, who was sick, who'd bought cattle or sold land. She told me everything so I'd feel a part of things. But she never talked about the movie. You know why?"

I clamped my teeth over my lips and shook my head.

"It's nothing bad. Don't look so scared. I made a fool of myself is all. It was a week before the filming was due to end. I know because your mother had marked it on the calendar for me so I could come home as soon as they left if I felt steady enough. For a couple of months your granddad and some of the other ranchers had been losing calves to a mountain lion. Late one night the cattle started bellowing, and I could hear them running. I grabbed my rifle and tore out of the house. I guess I was still half asleep. I fell somehow. The damned gun flew out of my hands and went off. The bullet went through my right shoulder and shattered my collar bone. I managed to start the pickup and drive one-handed to your granddad's. He drove me to the hospital. I had surgery the next morning. The day after that your granddad picked me up and took me home with him. I could tell by his face that he more than halfway didn't believe it was an accident. He thought my depression had got the better of me and I'd tried to kill myself and messed it up. I didn't want your mother thinking the same, so I made him promise not to tell her. That meant I had to stay at his house until the shoulder mended. He and your grandmother watched me the way Willie there watches a bird. Staying in the house like that took all my will power, but I felt like I had to prove to Doyle that I was okay. So, because of the shoulder, I stayed away longer than I should have. Your mother was real quiet when I got home. I know I hurt her, staying away so long. But I didn't want her worrying over me any more than she already had to. Your mother always took good care of me. She was more patient than any man had a right to expect."

Four days, Mott the reporter had said. Trejo had been found dead four days before the filming was finished. My father and I are not demonstrative, but I got up, bent over, and hugged him in sheer relief at knowing that when Jacinto Trejo had been murdered, he'd been confined to my grandfather's house.

TWENTY

On the drive home I thought about the various reactions to Jacinto Trejo's murder. It had troubled Tom Putnam because, having liked the man, the manner of Trejo's death had brought Tom's judgment into question. After retrieving a body over which they had no jurisdiction, the law had given the killing the most cursory investigation, merely asking witnesses to come forward. Jon French had paid for the *villista*'s funeral out of a sense of guilt and more probably with an eye to good public relations. No family had come forward to mourn the dead man. The only person who had grieved for Trejo had been my mother, and that in private.

The talk with my father had lessened the sense of betrayal, the feelings of resentment and loss that had been building since I read her journal. Had my father known, had he been hurt, I might have reacted differently. If Trejo had been another kind of man, taking advantage of my mother's loneliness, I might have hated him. But even Rosalinda Pray had seen the sincerity of Trejo's feelings. And I would have bet she was an expert when it came to dealing with insincerity. Trejo was dead, my mother was dead, yet I wanted to make it up to her for losing him, and for my resentment.

There were thirty-eight people in Polvo who had been extras in the movie. Eliminate those of my age, too young to have been aware of adult machinations, and that left thirteen people I could ask about what they remembered. Plus Hap Boyer, who had seen the body. Plus the locals who had hosted the actors during their stay.

When I arrived home, Chris and Clay were seated at the kitchen table discussing a time frame for Rosalinda Pray's visit to Cinco's.

"So tomorrow is okay with you?" Chris was saying as I dropped my keys on the counter.

"She'll have to understand that everything is off if I get an emergency call," Clay said firmly.

I nodded at them and went to the bedroom to make a telephone call. Dennis Bustamante answered on the first ring.

"I was going to call you," he said. "I checked around to see if anyone else had seen a person in a ghillie suit along that part of the river. A Border Patrol agent said an illegal he picked up told a story about something inhuman that rose up out of the scrub and chased him. The agent said that the guy was so scared he was begging to go back to Mexico."

"When was this?"

"From what the Mexican told him, it was the day after your friends saw it." There was the sound of papers being shuffled. "Anything else I can do for you?"

"A favor," I said. "Do you have access to old case files?"

"How old are we talking about?"

"Nineteen sixty-one."

"Jacinto Trejo."

"Dennis, are you psychic?"

"You're the second person today to ask about that file. The first was a writer named Carmondy. I'll tell you what I told him. If the body hadn't been found on No Man's Land, I'd say the file would still be around somewhere in old open cases since the statute of limitations never runs out on murder. But this? The file could have been thrown out. I'll see what I can do. Now you tell me something. Why all the sudden interest in a forty-year-old murder? Carmondy spun me some tale about gathering background for a story on the video and Pancho Villa's curse. So why are you interested?"

"Would you believe I want to exorcise a ghost?"

TWENTY-ONE

Chris had left. Clay stood in the kitchen slicing brisket, a bottle of barbecue sauce near at hand. He used the knife to slide the meat from the cutting board into a pan, put the pan into the oven, set the timer for fifteen minutes.

"I love a man who can heat up a meal," I said.

"Had a good visit with Justice, I take it?" Clay said, washing his hands at the sink.

I told him about it while I made the iced tea.

"Good. No more worries."

When the timer went off, he took the pan from the oven, sliced an onion, drained dill pickle slices from the jar, and heated hamburger buns in the microwave. After he opened the buns and spread barbecue sauce on them, he piled on the meat, pickles, and onions. I put ice in the glasses and poured tea. Clay brought the sandwiches and napkins to the table.

"By the way," Clay said as he sat down, "have you joined

the Texas National Guard?" He pointed to the ghillie suit still draped over one of the chairs where I'd left it.

"Sounds like we have a serious poacher around," he said after I'd explained. "I'll call the game warden."

"I meant to tell Dennis about finding it, but I had other things on my mind."

"When did you talk to Dennis?"

That required another explanation, and by the time I had made it we were finished with our sandwiches.

As we carried our dirty plates and glasses to the sink Clay said, "I want you to think long and hard about opening up this business about Trejo."

"I think Mr. Carmondy may have beaten me to it anyway."

"Let him," Clay said. "I don't like seeing you upset the way you were last night. Sometimes it's better to let the past go."

"Right now I feel like it's the past doing the holding on."

We washed the dishes together. "I'm going to take a nap," I announced, wiping the drain with the dish towel.

"Look at this." Clay stood by the table holding the pants of the ghillie suit up to himself, the waist at his waist. "Whoever the poacher is, he's taller than me by about . . ." His face grew long. ". . . a good four inches." He held the pants away, looking as if he didn't believe what he saw. "What is Hugh Wesleco doing creeping around in this getup?" His tone was puzzled.

"We don't know that belongs to Hugh just because—"

"How many people do we know around here who are six-foot-five?" Clay demanded. "Anyone else wearing this would be tripping over his feet." He looked down to the pants dragging the floor, then back at me. I didn't respond right away because I was thinking of Hugh buying the Whole Growth feed, Hugh knowing all about the Mexican village site.

"One of us had better talk to him," Clay said. "Find out what's going on."

That's the border way. As much as possible, we handle our own problems.

TWENTY-TWO

A pack rat carrying something in its teeth scuttled around the corner of the trading post as I went to my pickup. No doubt the burn debris was being used by any number of the creatures for nest building. Now that the investigator had done his work, I could get things cleaned up.

It was a little after seven, and the sky was growing light. The cool winds that rise in the evening and blow all night had died down. The trees along the river were filled with chattering birds. Overhead two loud crows chased a mockingbird away from their territory.

At 3:00 A.M. Clay had performed emergency surgery on a local man's injured dog, and he was now sleeping late. I had left the answering machine on to take his calls and set the alarm to wake him in time to go with Chris to meet Rosalinda Pray at Cinco's.

Last evening I had telephoned Hugh at the ranch, but had

gotten no answer. My second telephone call had been to Tom Putnam, who I was now on my way to see.

It was still dark when I drove past Polvo, setting all the dogs to barking. Five miles farther along the graded road that the government had tried so unsuccessfully to lengthen and improve, I turned off, threading my way across a narrow, sandy wash, past stunted mesquite and catclaw, and onto the ranch road beyond. By the time I reached the headquarters of the Lazy Ace Ranch, the sky was a sun-drenched blue.

Tom Putnam was dressed in a light gray shirt and darker slacks. Only his stooping shoulders gave away his age. His hand clasp was warm and friendly, and he invited me to join him for coffee. I followed him through the spacious living room, through French doors, and onto the flagstone patio looking out over the pasture that stretched to the east side of what was known as Goat Mountain, its slopes dotted with scattered gray oaks and limestone scree. The glass-topped table was set for two with fresh fruit, rolls, and a silver coffeepot.

He poured the coffee. I helped myself to cream and accepted a warm homemade cinnamon roll from the napkin-wrapped basket he held out. Tom employed the best cook in the whole of the Trans-Pecos.

"I heard about the fire," he said, picking up the napkin that the light breeze had lifted from the table. "Are things getting back to normal for you?"

I gave him an abbreviated account, we chatted about his family, and finally I broached the subject that had brought me to his house.

Tom was too polite to ask why I was curious about Jacinto Trejo's death when I asked him if he recalled whether the *villista* was preoccupied or upset.

Tom thought about it. "He was . . . quiet. I put that down to the argument he had with Jon French."

"When was this?"

"Maybe two days before Trejo was found dead. I'd been out to the barn to check on a motherless calf one of the hands had brought in from the pasture. When I came back, I could hear Trejo and French arguing right there in the living room. French was shouting. Something like, 'I said I'd take care of it and I will. Give me time.' Then Trejo said, 'You're out of time,' or, 'There is no more time.' There was something more about putting a stop to it himself. When I walked in, they hushed up, but Trejo looked furious and his hand was balled up in a fist." Tom fingered the copper bracelet he wore for arthritis. "I think if I hadn't come in when I did, Trejo would have taken a swing at French."

"Did either of them offer an explanation?"

"Not a word," Tom said. "Trejo walked out. French looked downright sick. He sat down for a few minutes, then left to view the rushes. Whatever the fuss was about, it sure changed their relationship. They hardly spoke after that. I always thought French felt guilty after Trejo died. I figured that's why he jumped in before anybody else had the chance and offered to pay for the funeral."

I stayed with Tom for another half-hour while he told me eveything he could remember about the last week of Trejo's life, but nothing seemed significant. Or if it was, I didn't know enough to appreciate it.

I was halfway home before I decided to take the cutoff and go to Cinco's. I didn't know when or if I would see Rosalinda Pray again, and I had a question for her. The road climbed for sixteen slow, bumpy miles, forded a dry creek, and then dropped sharply into the shallow valley where the *ranchito* lay.

The yard was jammed with four-wheel-drive vehicles that belonged to friends of Cinco's who had come to help him in an all-day doctoring session with the horses. In one corral the cowhands vaccinated and marked the horses with numbered bands. In another Clay and Cinco gelded the stallion, making him easier to work with and more adoptable.

Rosalinda Pray sat in an old garden chair nearby where she could watch. She wore a western shirt patterned like a Navajo blanket, tight jeans, and red boots. As I approached she took off the designer sunglasses and gave me a smile that made me think she was genuinely glad to see me.

She patted the arm of the chair next to her. "Sit. This has been an amazing morning. Your husband is a treasure to put up with me like this, though I do think he was hard on poor Pippa. She nips at every animal she meets."

"Did she bite at the horses?"

"Yes. Clay grabbed her, and she peed on him." Rosalinda made a pouty mouth. "He locked her in the barn."

"It's for her own safety," I said. "Even sick horses can kick."

"I almost cried when I saw those poor animals," Rosalinda said, her soprano voice rising even higher. "Clay tells me they already look better than the day they arrived here. That's hard to imagine."

I nodded. "They've put on a few pounds, and their eyes are brighter."

"Cinco says in six more weeks they'll look like different animals. He's so . . . real. Down-to-earth, like you and Clay. I can't imagine why he wouldn't agree to let me publicize all this for him. I think I'd make a great spokesperson. Maybe you could talk him into it?"

"Maybe," I said. I wanted her to stay sweet to answer my questions. "Rosalinda—"

"Rosy."

"Rosy. I need some information. During the last couple of weeks of filming *Panchito,* did you notice any change in Jacinto Trejo's behavior?"

"Like what?"

"Anything odd. Anything out of character. Any awkwardness between him and anyone else? Or arguments."

"Is this about his murder?"

I looked across to the corral. One of the cowboys was rubbing down a horse's legs with liniment. Clay was washing his hands in a bucket of soapy water, and Cinco was putting out fresh hay. The work was about done, and Clay would be ready to go home. I turned back to Rosalinda. "Yes. Do you remember anything?"

"Texana, we reported for makeup at five in the morning. We didn't finish shooting until five in the afternoon. In the evenings we watched the rushes. By the last ten or fourteen days of shooting we were all irritable." She paused. "Even Jon French showed the strain. His ulcer flared up, and he started chewing antacid tablets like gum. But no, I don't remember anything particular." She paused and gave me a sideways look. "Forgive me, but Jacinto's preoccupation—might it have been because he didn't know how to say good-bye to your mother?"

"I've thought of that myself. But there is that niggling little fact that somebody killed him."

She reached out and put her hand on my arm. "It was a long time ago. What can you find out? And what good would it do?"

"Probably none," I agreed. I heard the corral gate shut. Clay joined us. He expressed no surprise, though I knew he must have wondered why I'd made a long detour to get here. I said good-bye to Rosalinda, told Clay I'd see him at home, and walked to my pickup.

When I got home, I went to work clearing some of the debris from the explosion. I started at the burned-out motor home. After filling five thirty-three-gallon garbage bags, I hadn't progressed much further. I felt the same way about solving Jacinto Trejo's murder.

TWENTY-THREE

I was back at my garbage-collecting job the next morning. The bags would be taken away by a man from across the river who would sort through them for anything he could salvage.

At ten Nellie came out of the motor home, dressed in a red T-shirt stretched over bulging muscles, white jogging shorts, and serious running shoes. I admired the man for his discipline. Except for the day of the fire and explosion, the nurse hadn't missed a single daily run. As he turned onto the road, he threw up a hand in greeting to the driver of the Ram Charger slowing to turn in.

Dennis Bustamante parked in the back lot. I tied off the garbage bag I was using and went to see what had brought the deputy all this way. The manila folder in his hand gave me a clue.

"If that's the murder file on Trejo, you work fast," I said, stripping off my gloves and stuffing them into the back pocket of my jeans.

"It's not a murder file, since it was never an official case. It's just a few notes the sheriff made in case anything showed the victim died somewhere other than No Man's Land. Obviously that never happened, since he never opened an official investigation."

"Let's go inside."

We sat at the table. He pushed the file across to me.

To look at, the folder might have been empty. It almost was. There was a page and a half of notes, written forty years ago.

"Mind if I make myself a cup of coffee?" Dennis asked.

"Everything is on the counter," I said absently.

By the time Dennis had his cup of coffee, I had finished reading. Three little boys who'd floated a *chalupa*—river Spanish for a homemade boat—out to No Man's Land had found the body at the waterline of the narrow end of the tiny island, face up, half in and half out of the river. They had rowed back to the U.S. side and run home. Their mother had called the sheriff's office in Marfa. Shorthanded then as now, the sheriff, a man named Warren House, had contacted the Border Patrol to ask if agents in the area could check out the island and make sure the kids hadn't panicked over a pile of trash or a dead animal. Agents Abelardo Segura and Hap Boyer had at first assumed they had a floater that had washed up until they saw the crushed skull and the blood-matted hair on the left side of the head. Even without jurisdiction, they had accepted that they would have to retrieve the body. They had searched the dead man's pockets and found a Mexican driver's license, 156 dollars in cash, a handkerchief, and a small notebook with the names and addresses of Jon French, Tom Putnam, and the Ricciotti Trading Post. They had notified the sheriff's office.

"Want a cup?" I looked up from my reading to Dennis's attentive face. He held the coffeepot. I shook my head and looked at a notation, written on the back of one of the pages, about Trejo's pickup being found by the cops in Ojinaga.

I looked up at Dennis sitting across from me drinking his coffee. "Why isn't there more information? I thought there'd be witness statements, things like when he was last seen, whether anybody reported him missing."

"Like I said, there was no case officially. The body wasn't found in U.S. territory, and there was no evidence he was killed here. There wasn't even an autopsy. The county wasn't going to pay for an investigation that they couldn't take to court."

"What about the truck being found?"

"Trejo must have driven over here in his own truck," Dennis said. "Sometime after the murder I guess it turned up on the other side. Probably the sheriff tried to hand the whole mess over to Mexico. But they weren't interested either."

I turned back to the first page and scanned it. There was something that wasn't right, but what? I closed the file and handed it to Dennis, thanking him.

Dennis tapped his finger on the file. "What's your interest in this man's death?"

Omitting my mother's personal relationship with Trejo, I told him the truth—that I had found a journal my mother kept about the filming in which she noted Jacinto Trejo's preoccupation in the days leading up to his murder and that it had made me curious. I don't think he believed that was all there was to it, but he didn't say so.

"I hear Miss Masters is improving," Dennis said, topping up his coffee.

"That's good news." I felt guilty that I hadn't been to visit Gwen in the hospital.

I got up to answer the telephone. It was Sixta Ramos, and her voice was angry. "Is Jimmy there pestering that Mr. Anthony again?" I told her I'd check and call her back.

"Jimmy Ramos is cutting school again," I explained to Dennis. He picked up the file and came outside with me.

"I'll keep an eye out for the kid," he said, getting into his car.

I knocked on the RV door. Nellie hadn't seen the boy.

"I'm going to walk that boy to and from the school bus

every day for the rest of this year," Sixta said when I called her back.

Poor Sixta. I knew the truant officer had warned her about Jimmy's absences, threatening to jail her if the boy had many more.

I collected an empty garbage bag and went outside. Polveños came and went from taping sessions while I worked. By the time Clay ended his morning clinic hours, I had cleared the RV lot.

Clay was in the shower when I went inside. When he came out, I took my turn, washing away the grime of the cleanup and changing into fresh clothes. I put the soot-streaked ones into the washer.

"How does tuna salad sound for lunch?" I asked him when I got to the kitchen, opened the refrigerator, and found nothing especially inspiring.

"It always tastes better than it sounds," he said.

I got out a bag of walnuts, two cans of tuna, an apple, an onion, an avocado, and the mayonnaise. "You haven't said a word about Rosalinda Pray's reaction when Cinco said no to her publicity campaign."

"She tried to talk Cinco into changing his mind. If she'd used her head and hadn't been so pushy, he'd have probably agreed. He approves of Chris's video. But he read Rosalinda Pray exactly right. The only thing she's interested in promoting is herself. I don't think Cinco appreciated being used."

"She told me she was hoping for television work after Scott's video comes out. I gather she's a bit desperate for some success. Actually, I rather like her. There's no pretense about her anyway."

Clay lifted a walnut half out of the salad and popped it in his mouth. "It's like being around an emu. She's always squeaking and running all over the place."

After lunch, Clay left to run errands in Presidio, taking with him my bank deposit and an order for rolls of nickels, dimes, and quarters for the register. Pesos I had in plenty.

After he left, I tried calling Hugh again, but there was still no answer. I knew I should finish the parking lot cleanup, but instead I took a break and went to sit on the front porch. In the RV lot, Nellie, long back from his run and equipped with a stepladder and a bucket of soapy water, was cleaning the RV's windows. There's nothing so pleasant as watching someone else work knowing that you don't have to join in. Eventually Nellie folded the ladder, dumped out the dirty water, and went back inside. Polveños came and went at regular intervals for tapings, each stopping to catch me up on the news. Belia Luna had celebrated her first communion. Coyote Barker had fallen asleep at the wheel driving back from Marfa and totaled his car. Three houses at Shafter had been broken into while the owners were at work. Joe Galindo had visited from San Antonio, bringing his mother a microwave oven. It was Tomás Ramos, brother-in-law of Sixta and grandson of Lucy, the postmistress, who brought the news that Hugh Wesleco had let his ranch hands go with two weeks extra pay, and Jerry Ayrs had hired them for the Black Buzzard ranch.

The news about Hugh astonished me. Ranch hands came and went, usually back and forth across the border, but Hugh's men had been, as far as I knew, experienced and trustworthy. What was going on with my old friend?

By five-thirty I began wondering what was taking Clay so long in town.

I was about to end my porch sitting and think about dinner when a flame-red pickup with the Virgin of Guadalupe painted in bright colors on the hood turned in and parked in front of the porch. There was a strong family resemblance in the faces of the two people on the front seat: Paco Combs, a shaggy-haired young man with an engaging grin, and his grandmother, Eva Ybarra.

He opened his door, stepped out, said "Hiya" to me, walked around, and opened the passenger door. Eva got out. Paco slammed the door shut, then hurried to take her arm, saying, "Lemme help you, Grandma." Eva looked exasperated but let him hold her arm as she told him she would sit on the porch. She pointed her cane at one of the chairs. I steadied it as she sat down.

"Texana, I want to show you something." She took an object out of her pocket and held it out to me.

"Remember at the party in Presidio I told you about the gift Dane Anthony gave Felita in nineteen-sixty-one? This is the *relicario*. Isn't it lovely?"

The large religious locket was unexpectedly thick and heavy in my hand. The chain and the frame were silver. The image carved on the ivory face of the locket was a lamb, a halo around its head, a shepherd's staff protruding from between its forelegs. It was the *Agnus Dei*, the Lamb of God.

"At the first taping," Eva said, "I told the story about the gift, and Scott asked if I could bring it to show on camera, so I called my daughter in San Antonio. She had Paco bring it to me."

"I had to swear I wouldn't let it out of my sight the whole way," Paco said, "so I wore it around my neck. Kept it under my shirt at truck stops. It looks a little girly, you know."

"I think I've seen this before," I said.

"Felita probably showed it to you," she said. "That girl never let it out of her hand for three or four days after Dane gave it to her. Then I took it to the jeweler to have a chain made for it. He told me the *relicario* was very old, made before the revolution. He said that a wealthy family, *haciendados,* would have owned it and that it had considerable value. After that, I made Felita put it away until she was older."

Paco said, "Mom has only told that story a million times about the big Hollywood star coming to her fifteenth birthday celebration."

Jenna came out to the porch. "Scott's ready for you." Paco went with them.

I stayed on the porch, reliving the memory triggered by seeing the locket. Jacinto Trejo had been going to put me on the horse so my mother could take my picture, the one in the album. He bent down to lift me up, and the locket fell out of his shirt pocket. I picked it up and looked at it. I liked the lamb. Then I handed it back to him.

I waited until Eva came back out and asked her to let me look at the locket again.

"Hey," Paco said, "show her what's inside. There's a lock of hair. Mom would never let us kids touch the locket, but she showed us the hair. A relic, she called it, cut from the head of a saint."

Eva opened the locket and handed it to me. A coil of light brown hair rested against a white backing. It was the color of my mother's hair. A match for the lock I had in the box in the closet.

"I always thought it was probably a *chinito,*" Eva was saying. "From a child's first haircut. My grandmother had a *relicario,* not so nice as this. She kept hair from each of her children in it."

I gave the locket back to her. She snapped it shut and slipped it into her pocket. Paco took her arm as she started down the steps. I walked with them and watched as they drove away. Eva had been Scott's last taping session for the day. I went to our living quarters. Maybe the locket was only similar to the one I had glimpsed as a child, and the color of the lock of hair a coincidence. But I knew now what it was about the sheriff's report that had bothered me: the list of the contents of Trejo's pockets. Tom Putnam had told a story at the dinner party in Presidio, too. Something about a good luck charm that Trejo had carried. Nothing like that had been on the list. But I had seen the *relicario* Trejo carried in his pocket. Was that the good luck charm? What had happened to it?

I had my hand on the telephone, intending to call Tom Putnam, when it rang. It was Jose Reyes.

"Jimmy Ramos is missing."

TWENTY-FOUR

I dressed warmly and carried a heavy jacket for when the dark set in. Hypothermia is the danger of desert nights. I laced up my walking boots, got my flashlight, then went to the front. The thick, trailing electrical cords and the arc lamps of the staging area looked out of place in a setting that hadn't changed much since the turn of the century. I would be glad when things were back to normal and the place was solely mine once again. I locked the front doors, then got an empty cardboard box from the stack at the end of the counter. I packed flashlights and packages of batteries to hand out to those who would be searching on foot. Most searchers in pickups, especially the ranchers, would have spotlights, useful when looking for strayed or sick animals, which go off by themselves, and for hunting nocturnal predators like mountain lions, which could decimate a herd of its calves. Or kill a little boy. I hurried. We had to find Jimmy quickly.

I jammed the pistol I keep for rattlesnakes into the back

pocket of my jeans. It would be too cold for snakes, but there were other dangers along the river at night. Even small-time drug smugglers came armed these days. I wrote a note for Clay and propped it against the salt shaker on the table.

Before I left, I knocked on the door of the RV to ask Dane whether Jimmy Ramos had been hanging around today, but neither he nor Nellie had seen the boy. Nor had any of the crew, who were gathered around Jeremy's small outdoor grill cooking burgers. I told them that the boy had cut school, was not yet home, and, if they saw him, to call the church.

The church adjoins the cemetery in Polvo, and judging from the number of vehicles double- and triple-parked around both, a funeral might have been under way. I parked far enough along the road to guarantee I wouldn't be blocked in and walked to the meeting.

The wooden doors of the small adobe church had been propped open, and the entry was crowded with people whose faces had the look of suppressed excitement and solemnity that accompanies the possibility of tragedy.

I was greeted with silent nods by the men and women hovering in the doorway because a middle-aged man in front of the altar rail was addressing the people filling the pews and leaning against the walls beneath the stations of the cross. I put down the box of flashlights to listen to what Ruben Reyes, Jose's son, was saying.

"Benito's group will fan out from here to the trading post, working north, away from the river. My group will take the road from here to the cave-in, again moving north. Salvador's group will work the riverbank. Please walk within sight of each other. That way we won't overlook him. It's better if you're too close together than too far apart."

"Have you called the Border Patrol?" someone asked.

"They're sending a helicopter and a couple of units. The sheriff's men are bringing horses. The high school kids will be checking outbuildings again. We're going to ask you to sign up for one of the three search groups so we can balance the numbers. Anybody with four-wheel drive, see me."

The lines formed down the center aisle and to either side along the wall. I picked up the box of flashlights and walked to the front, set it down on the altar rail, and pointed it out to one of the organizers, Asuncion Loya, who had a barber chair in the front yard of her house and gave haircuts for five dollars.

"Good thinking. We'll put them in the middle where folks can get them."

"I have four-wheel drive," I said.

"Ruben, bring the map," she called. Ruben came over with a geological survey map and pointed to Frio Draw, one of a series of gullies that drain the rimrock.

"Can you take this one? We're thinking, when it gets cold, he'll try and get out of the wind," Ruben said. "It'll be in the thirties tonight."

"And no moon," Asuncion said.

"Do we know what Jimmy was wearing?" I asked.

"He had on a bright blue windbreaker, jeans, and white tennis shoes. Sixta couldn't remember the color of his shirt."

"Is anyone checking around Presidio? Maybe he got off the school bus and went somewhere in town."

"His brother Joe says he cut out before the school bus got here this morning. The truant officer came to his class and asked Joe, but he didn't tell because he didn't want to be a *chismoso*."

Tattletale. Who wants to rat on a friend or a brother? I thought of Hugh and the possibility that he was the poacher in the ghillie suit and felt a comradeship with Jimmy's brother. But the consequences of loyalty had to be lived with. I hoped for both our sakes that we hadn't misused ours.

Ruben penciled in my name by Frio Draw, and I left for my pickup.

Even with the headlights on bright, the slopes seemed to absorb the light. I used a spotlight plugged into the cigarette lighter to sweep the rocky area and drove with the window down so I could honk periodically and listen for an answer. For once I did not enjoy the silence. I thought of the dangers. Mountain lion, the cold, even javelina, whose tusks could pierce flesh. More than once Clay had stitched up a large dog injured by the nearly blind creatures with an acute sense of smell. What might they do to a boy?

I heard the helicopter long before the intense circle of white light captured the pickup and turned a thirty-foot swath of the draw into day before moving on. The Border Patrol was still searching.

It had taken me forty minutes to travel five miles. At that, I had gone much farther than a small boy on foot could have. I managed, by backs and starts, to turn the pickup and head back through the black night. Above my head the individual stars were blazingly bright, but the Twins and Dogs and Hunters were useless to my quest. I would have given much for moonlight.

By the time I returned to the church most of the searchers had come in, each hoping the next person to return would bring the child. Surrounded by family, Sixta sat in a front pew before the figure of Our Lady, her fingers moving over the beads of the rosary, her lips repeating the Hail Mary down the decades, finding comfort in ritual, hope in faith.

"We'll start again at daylight," Ruben said, his voice spirited, his face defeated.

I trudged back to my pickup to find Clay's green truck parked behind me. I waited for him. "When did you get back from Presidio?" I asked when he arrived.

"Around seven-thirty. The mayor wanted to talk about the stray dog problem. I found your note and came straight here."

"Where did you search?" I asked.

"The road's end. The engineers left a lot of junk when they tried to extend the road, and the kids like to play there."

"It's too bad one of the Border Patrol trackers didn't get

to look for signs before everybody tramped all over the place," I said.

We drove home on a road as empty as our luck had been.

Scott, Chris, and Nellie hurried over as soon as we parked. "A helicopter with a spotlight has been all over the place," Scott said. "Is it the kid they're searching for or has something else happened?"

Clay explained. "We've done about all we can with a foot search. Everybody with a horse and saddle will be out tomorrow," Clay told them.

We said good-night.

The trading post had never seemed less welcoming, so empty. I missed the bobcat's presence. We washed our hands, then made a quick meal of cheese and crackers. Before we went to bed Clay checked his messages.

"This is Pat. My dog pulled a pan of lasagna off the stove and ate it. Will it hurt him?" "Clay, Randy Burack. I've shipped your order." "Clay, one of the kid's ponies is lame. Can you come out tomorrow?" "Cinco here. I'm missing one of those bottles of antibiotic you gave me."

TWENTY-FIVE

Hugh let Jake and Gus go?" Clay said. "I need to check with them. I was hoping they might have picked up that missing bottle of antibiotic with their gear when they helped us rescue the horses. If they're at Jerry's, like you say, I'll call him before I leave. Why would Hugh fire good ranch hands right before cattle roundup time?"

I poured syrup over my waffles. "Beats me. But that's what I was told. Something's going on with him. When things settle down around here, I'll go and see him."

"When I suggested that one of us should talk to him about whether or not he'd been roaming the river in a ghillie suit, I had in mind a telephone call."

"I've tried," I said. "If he's home, he's not answering the telephone."

"I might be able to swing by when I'm out on a call and have a talk with him," Clay said.

"I'll do it. I've known him since we were kids. He used to play with me and my friends. Until he changed."

"How so?"

"He stopped hanging around with us. He'd come to school and go home. He didn't seem to want any friends." I tipped the carton of half-and-half and turned my coffee white. "And something's going on with him now."

"Whatever it is," Clay said, "I don't think it's poaching, in spite of the ghillie suit. Maybe Jenna was right. Maybe he has gone survivalist. Maybe he's stockpiling weapons and cans of soup."

The telephone rang. It was the man who'd left the message about the lame pony. Clay told him he'd be there by eight, then disconnected and called Jerry.

"What are you going to do today?" he asked me, after leaving a message on Jerry's answer machine.

"Hang around here and wait for news about Jimmy."

Clay finished his breakfast then got his coat. "Call me if you hear anything."

He stopped halfway out the door. "Remember, the Border Patrol will be searching. They may not know you're closed for the tapings. Better post a sign, or they might walk in and ruin the audio."

I was printing the sign when he popped back in and dropped something on the table in front of me.

"I bought that in Presidio yesterday. I thought you'd get a kick out of it," he said, looking over my shoulder as I read the tabloid headline: "Brave Rosy Battles Pancho Villa's Ghost." A photograph showed Rosalinda Pray fighting off a whispy white figure in a sombrero.

"Gee, do you think they faked the picture?" Clay said as he left.

I had the notice posted by the time Scott and the crew went to work. After that, I made the bed and cleaned the bathroom, thinking all the while of Jimmy. He was a smart kid, but a loner. He'd cut school many times. But he'd never before failed to come home by the time the school bus dropped off the other kids. To stop worrying, I made myself think of something else while I dusted the furniture. Trejo and Felita's *relicario*. My memory of seeing it, or one very similar, was sharp. I finished dusting, then went to telephone Tom Putnam.

I asked if he had heard about Hugh letting his hands go. He expressed surprise. "They're good workers, those two. I can't imagine what Hugh's thinking. Unless the Weslecos have decided to sell out. I know Holmes and Estefina talked about it when they moved to El Paso after Holmes's heart attack. Hugh is the only one of their children with an interest in ranching."

Tom asked if there was news of the missing boy. His three ranch hands were helping with horseback search. "I'd be out with them," he said, "if my eyes weren't so bad."

We talked about how he was coping with the macular degeneration that was slowly robbing him of his peripheral vision. Then I came around to the reason for my call. "You mentioned something at the party in Presidio about a good luck charm that Jacinto Trejo wore."

"Yes," Tom said. "To protect him from the devil and disaster. I liked his turn of phrase. In his own way, Trejo was eloquent."

"This charm, what did it look like?"

"I never actually saw it. Whatever it was," Tom added, "it should have been on his body. I packed up his things myself afterward. Gave the suitcase to the sheriff. There was nothing but his clothes and toiletries."

His answer brought my quest to a dead end. After I hung up, I called Hap Boyer, but the retired Border Patrol agent wasn't at home. Probably out with the searchers. I checked the directory for the man who'd been Hap's partner. In twenty-six pages of listings, the West of the Pecos telephone book covers thirty-three communities in five counties, a testament to our sparse population. No Abelardo Segura.

If I was right, and the *relicario* I remembered had been

Trejo's good luck charm, it could have been taken by any number of people: the children who'd found the body, one of the agents, someone in the Sheriff's Department. Or the killer. And there might be a simple explanation for why the *relicario* I had seen looked so much like the one given to Eva's daughter by Dane Anthony. If someone took it from the body, he might have sold it. Sold it to someone with ready cash, someone who would be leaving the area soon, a plus in case the *relicario* was reported missing. Someone like Dane Anthony. There was one way to find out.

As I walked to the motor home I spotted a rider on the hill behind the trading post, the horse picking its way through the Spanish dagger, ocotillo, and other prickly plants on the stony soil. The search was still on.

Nellie let me in. He wore a chef's apron over his knit shirt and jeans. He closed the door behind me. Dane was already smiling a welcome. Nellie went to the kitchen. I heard chopping.

In the living area the CD player was on. There was a book on the table beside the actor's chair, a western, judging by the cover.

"Is there news of little Jimmy?" he asked. My answer seemed to genuinely distress him. "The young are so precious."

I glanced at the book. "Did I interrupt your reading?"

"I'm thinking of optioning the book for a movie."

"Does that mean you'll give up your television show?"

"Not at all. Last month I signed for another season. No, the television show is the best thing to happen to my career. Its success is opening all sorts of doors. But I would enjoy a project that was all mine. I want to produce and direct."

"Like Jon French in *Panchito,*" I said.

"Yes."

"You were one of the executive producers, weren't you?"

"A courtesy title. I had no input. If I had, the movie might have had more success." He called for Nellie to make coffee.

"None for me, thanks," I said.

"Eva Ybarra is one of our locals who was an extra in the movie," I said.

The actor murmured, "Of course."

"She showed me a beautiful antique *relicario* that you gave her daughter for a birthday present."

"Did I?"

"It was a momentous event for Eva and her daughter. With the *relicario*'s religious significance, it was the perfect gift for a girl's *quinceañera.* In Hispanic culture a fifteenth birthday is a coming-of-age event. I'm so curious. Where did you find the *relicario*?"

He looked blank. "You caught me. I don't recall the gift. What did you call it?"

"A *relicario.* Ivory set in silver with a carving on the front. A lamb."

His face brightened. "The locket! I got it in Ojinaga. An impulse buy. Afterward, I couldn't imagine what I'd do with it, so I gave it to the young lady."

TWENTY-SIX

Clay came home at eleven-thirty, looking tired and pale, as if he was coming down with something. He confirmed that when he took two cold and flu capsules with lunch. While I washed the dishes, he checked his messages. Jerry Ayrs had asked the ranch hands. No one knew anything about the missing bottle of antibiotic.

"I guess I'll know who took it when some damned fool kills a horse with it," he said.

"If they don't read the label, it's their fault," I told him.

He stretched out on the couch and fell asleep.

The afternoon was interminably long. Two of the four people scheduled to be taped failed to show. I told Scott they were probably on the search team. The Border Patrol helicopter flew over more than once, and a light plane droned back and forth, flying so low I half expected it to be intercepted by the DEA.

As the hours passed and no word came, even the video crew grew long-faced and silent. Chris and Jenna and Scott and I sat on the porch and watched as one by one the search vehicles passed by on the way back to Presidio and Marfa. One turned in and stopped at the gas pumps.

"I was running on fumes," Dennis Bustamante said, coming up the steps while the tank filled.

"Any news?" Clay said.

The deputy shook his head. "Nothing. We tried Joe Ranger's dogs. They found the kid's scent all over the place, but every time it either ran out or led back to the bus turn-around."

"What next?"

"The official search is over. Some of the riders and neighbors will be out tomorrow. Father Mario is with the family."

Father Mario had replaced Father Jack Raff, who had lived among us for five years before being reassigned to an inner city parish in Chicago.

The pump clicked off, and Dennis went to hang up the hose, then followed me inside. While I rang up the sale, he said, "You remember what I told you about that Carmondy fellow calling me about the Trejo murder? Well, he called back, asking questions about the video bunch. Wanted to know if there'd been any problems of any sort while they were here. Those were his exact words, 'any problems of any sort.' Fishing without bait, as far as I was concerned. But I think he had something specific in mind, and he darn sure didn't want to give it away to me. Has there been any trouble?"

I gave him his credit card receipt. "Apart from the fire and explosion, nothing. The crew have been great. I like all of them."

I followed Dennis out to the porch and rejoined the others. After the deputy left, Nellie came across to ask about Jimmy on behalf of his boss, who'd seen the deputy from the window and hoped there might be good news. Scott and Jenna went to their RV. Chris remained on the porch talking to Clay. I half listened to the young man's questions about being a vet in such a remote area and my husband's answers, but my mind was on what Dennis had told me.

I went inside, looked up a number, and made a call. When the newspaper office in Marfa answered, I asked to speak to Mr. Mott. A woman's voice asked me to hold.

"Mott. What can I do for you?"

I explained what I wanted.

"I can do better than tell you what you want to know," he said. "What's your fax number?"

I cut the pages as they rolled out of the fax machine. The copy of Mott's article taken from the Alpine newspaper began with a capsule piece on the video, with several quotes from Scott, and included background on *Panchito,* its director and actors, and information about the video crew.

There wasn't that much that I hadn't already learned from talking with them. Scott and Chris, both from Austin, had worked together on a number of projects, including one short subject film that had won an award. Jenna had relocated to Texas from California, where she'd worked for a local radio station. This was her first project since joining Scott's video production team. Jeremy was mentioned as an independent photographer from California hired by the video firm.

Then there were the paragraphs about the movie, mostly a rehash of old information. One fact was new, at least to me: the explanation of Three Minds Production, which I remembered from the movie credits. French had financed the making of *Panchito* with his own money and that of his two partners, Rosalinda Pray and Dane Anthony. All of the same mind presumably.

I thought about it for a while, then I called Mott back and asked if he could tell me how to get in touch with Luther Carmondy.

TWENTY-SEVEN

The retired film critic turned freelance writer was staying at the Paisano Hotel in Marfa. His wheeze was more noticeable on the telephone. He wanted to talk with me in person. "I'll be there by ten tomorrow."

That left the rest of the evening for me to figure out exactly how much I wanted to tell him.

Clay was feeling worse and his stomach was upset, so I baked two potatoes and we had an early dinner. Afterward, he took two more cold and flu capsules and went to bed. I retrieved the lock of my mother's hair from the box of keepsakes, folded it in a handkerchief that I tucked into my pocket, and went to see Eva Ybarra.

In Polvo there are neither street signs nor streetlights. Everyone knows where everyone else lives, and the dangers do not come from our neighbors. On this night, with one of our own missing, lights burned in every home. That was unusual in a community that still rose with the dawn. Even the dogs seemed subdued, their barks perfunctory, but loud enough to bring faces to the windows in the hope that I might be someone bringing news of Jimmy. When I failed to stop at the Ramoses' house, the curtains fell limply back into place. At Eva's house, she, too, had been restlessly listening. When I stopped at her adobe, she flung the door open.

"Texana?"

"No news, Eva. Nothing bad. I need your help."

We sat in the tiny living room with its polished 1930s furniture. The top of an upright piano angled into one corner was covered with family portraits, pictures of the children who had practiced diligently or listlessly on its keys.

I omitted small talk and got straight to the point.

"Do you still have Felita's *relicario*?"

"Yes. Did you want to see it?"

"Please." As she went to get it I brought out the folded handkerchief.

She returned with the *relicario* and came forward to hand it to me, but I stopped her. "You open it," I said, "and compare this to the lock of hair inside." I folded back the top half of the handkerchief and placed it on the table beside her chair.

She sat down, opened the *relicario,* and gently took out the curled lock and placed it next to the other. She touched them.

"They're very like. The color, the texture and feel. Whose hair is this?" she asked.

"My mother's. Remember, as soon as the weather got hot in the spring, she'd cut it short."

"I remember," Eva said. She held up the lock of hair from the *relicario.* "Are you saying this is Sally's, too?"

I took a breath and slowly exhaled to calm myself. "When you showed me the *relicario,* I knew I'd seen it before. But it wasn't Felita who showed it to me. It was Jacinto Trejo."

I told about my memory of that day. "I found out that his *relicario* disappeared after his murder. Do you think it's possible that Felita's *relicario* is Trejo's and the lock of hair is my mother's?"

"It's possible. More than . . ." Concern showed so strongly in her face as she looked at me that I braced myself for something fearful. "You know the high regard I had for your mother," she said. "I don't know whether you were aware how lonely she felt. Your father's illness . . . it was very hard for her. Señor Trejo was a man of compassion."

"And a man of passion."

Eva looked startled. "You know?" she whispered.

"Mother left a journal in which she wrote about her relationship with him. You were her friend. I thought you might know. Did she tell you about it, or was it one of those open secrets, the kind everyone knows?"

"No. It was a gesture I saw her make. His collar was turned up on one side. She smoothed it down, and then her hand just lingered for a moment on his chest. It was a loving gesture."

The wind had picked up, and a draft was coming in from an open window. Eva went to close it. When she returned, she folded the handkerchief over the brown curl of hair and gave it back to me.

"Does this mean that Dane bought Felita a gift stolen from a dead man? That would mean bad luck."

I shook my head, feeling hopelessly confused. "I wish I knew more about what really happened," I said to myself as much as to Eva.

"Sometimes the more you know, the less you understand," she said quietly. I recognized the *dicho,* and I hoped Eva was wrong in applying it to this situation. It would have been hard to understand less than I did now.

TWENTY-EIGHT

Clay was feeling better and ate two poached eggs and toast for breakfast, showered, and went out to his clinic. Scott's first taping of the day was with Tom Putnam, and I wanted to have a word with the rancher before he left. Intending to sit in on the taping, I was heading to the front when someone knocked at the back door.

Jeremy was waiting for me, a stationery box in his hand.

"I thought the kid's family might want to make up some 'missing' posters," he said, handing me the box. I lifted the lid. Inside was a stack of black-and-white photographs of Jimmy Ramos, caught in a mischievous grin.

"So this is why I didn't see you all day yesterday," I said. Jeremy looked as if he'd caught the bug Clay had been fighting. His narrow face seemed thinner and the blue-gray shadows around his eyes darker.

"The kid was in a couple of the photographs I took of the crowd on the day of the group shoot. I enlarged the best one and cropped out the other people. I thought you'd know the best person to give them to."

I was touched by his thoughtfulness. "I'll get in touch with Ruben Reyes, who organized the local search. I think he's handling things for the family. By the way, I don't think I ever thanked you for how much help you were the day of the explosion, taking care of Ben's arm. You and Nellie were the heroes of the day. I don't know how you managed to stay so cool-headed."

"I used to work in a hospital to finance my photography. You pick up a few things."

"Useful things, I'd say. What kind of work did you do?"

"Boring work. I was a phlebologist, a fancy word for a technician who takes blood samples."

"It was a good thing for us that you knew what to do," I said.

After he left, I went to telephone Ruben about the photographs. "That's a big help," he said. "The sheriff asked for a picture to copy and distribute. I'll come get them."

I made it to the front in time to catch the last few seconds of Tom's reminiscences.

". . . one of my favorite memories. Early in the filming the Weslecos gave a dinner party for all the host families and their guests. My wife Nan and I drove Jon French and Jacinto Trejo to the party. We were the first to arrive. Holmes Wesleco showed us into the living room. There on the couch sat Mr. Anthony, with the Weslecos' little boy in his lap. He was totally absorbed, reading from *Treasure Island* in his most dramatic voice as if little Hugh was the most important audience in the world."

"Nice story, Mr. Putnam," Scott said, setting his clipboard aside and going over to unclip the microphone from Tom's collar. I moved from the doorway and called Tom's name. He smiled and turned toward me, placing me in his narrowed field of vision.

"Got a minute?" I asked. We walked into the back together. I had fresh coffee made, and I poured a cup, black with sugar, the way he liked it.

I placed the cup in front of him on the coffee table, then took the chair opposite. "Tom, I wanted to ask you a few more questions about Jacinto Trejo, if you don't mind. Would you tell me what you remember about the last time you saw him?"

"You know," he said, "you remind me of a Labrador I used to have. One scent and she was off on the trail. She didn't stop until she found what she was hunting." He drank some coffee. "Where's this scent leading you?"

"I'm not sure."

"Fair enough. Let's see if I can help. The last time I saw Trejo was at breakfast the day he disappeared. That was about seven. Jon French had left for the day's shooting by six. The actors had to be on the set by seven-thirty. Trejo usually went to watch the day's work. He drove to the set in an old blue Chevy pickup with bad brakes. He told me he was going to buy a new pickup after the movie was finished. I know he got to the set. French told me later, after the murder, that he remembered seeing him when they broke for lunch. When he didn't show up at the house for dinner, I didn't think anything about it because most nights French stayed late watching the rushes, and before their argument, Trejo would stay with him. They'd come back together after midnight. Nan kept the refrigerator stocked with ready-to-eat things so French and Trejo could help themselves. He wasn't at breakfast the next morning, but I figured he'd stayed with some of the crew playing poker."

"How long after the argument was it until he disappeared?"

He turned the cup in his hands, thinking. "Three days. That is, he wasn't at dinner on the third day."

"And how long after he disappeared before the body was found?"

"The next day. Sheriff House called around seven that evening. He said the Border Patrol had found Trejo dead."

I sat silent, thinking how bare-bones it all sounded. Tom asked, "Has any of this helped?"

I told him the truth. "I don't know yet."

It was nine-thirty. Scott had begun his next taping. I took myself and the box of photographs to the porch to wait for Ruben and for Carmondy.

TWENTY-NINE

The reporter arrived first, in a small rental car that looked as if it could barely contain his bulk. He took the steps slowly, pausing on each one to pull the portable oxygen cylinder up. I rose, intending to help, but he forestalled me with a raised hand. When he reached the porch level, he sat down heavily in the chair by the table, glancing down at the open box from which the likeness of Jimmy Ramos grinned up at him.

"Who's the kid?" Carmondy said.

"A local boy who's missing."

"By local, you mean around here? Not Presidio?"

"Jimmy's family lives in Polvo. His mother got him ready for school the day before yesterday and sent him off to catch the bus. He hasn't been seen since."

"Anything like this ever happen before around here?"

"No. Never."

He lifted the edge of the top photograph to get a better look. "Interesting. What is he, about nine, maybe ten?" He let the photograph fall back on the others and raised his eyes to mine. "You wanted to talk about Three Minds Production. What's your interest?"

"The night of Scott Regan's party I overheard you say that the only interesting thing about *Panchito* was the murder. You were talking about Jacinto Trejo's murder, weren't you?"

"I was."

"I agree with you. It's interesting. That's why I want to know about the production company . . ."

"And in return?"

"I know about an item that was missing from Trejo's body. I know who had it after the murder. I know where it is now."

"Fairly stuffed with information, aren't you?" His expression was neutral, but his eyes were interested. "Where shall I begin? Three Minds Production was Jon French, Dane Anthony, and Rosalinda Pray. French was a successful director, but by nineteen sixty his best films were behind him. The last movie he made before *Panchito* was a remake of *The Third Man* for Garner Studio. It went through three writers and came in over budget and long past the production deadline. Most of it ended up on the cutting room floor. The studio lost buckets of money and all confidence in French. Out of favor, he bought the rights to a book about Pancho Villa, wrote the script, and shopped for backers.

"Anthony was his first. He was in his late twenties. His acting career was on the upswing. He'd been a supporting actor in three hit movies and the star of one, for which he'd taken a smaller salary in return for a cut of the profits. Turned out to be a very good bet. It made him a wealthy man. He put in a sizable chunk toward financing *Panchito,* betting it would be another winner.

"Rosalinda Pray was an unknown with a few bit parts to her credit when she landed the role in *Panchito*. Cynical people like me said she bought the part with the cash divorce settlement she got from her first husband. She literally banked everything on the success of *Panchito*."

He wheezed to a stop and smiled winningly at me.
it's your turn to talk."

I outlined it for him. Trejo and Jon French had a ..
Someone had heard the director ask for more time, and Trejo answered that he would stop it, whatever "it" was. The island where the body later turned up had been the location of one of the first scenes in the movie to be filmed. Jon French had known that the island was the territory of neither Mexico nor the United States and had told at least one other person, Dane Anthony, about it. Because Trejo's body had been found on the island, the law on both sides of the river had done nothing to investigate the death. Trejo was known to have a good luck charm that hadn't been found on his body or in his room. Dane Anthony had given a birthday gift to a local child that I was confident was Trejo's good luck charm.

I deliberately left out my mother's journal and the lock of hair. And I knew Eva would be equally silent about the latter. I had to protect my father.

"Just vague enough to be interesting," he said when I finished. "So, assuming Trejo knew something that would have endangered the hoped-for success of the film, you're implying one of those three had a motive for murder."

"That's your inference. I'm just trying to follow where Jacinto Trejo takes me."

He stopped to take a breath and started coughing. For a long minute it was wheeze and cough, wheeze and cough. I asked if he needed some water, and he nodded.

When I returned with a bottle of water, his breathing was better, the coughing stopped. He gulped the water.

Ruben Reyes's white pickup stopped at the base of the steps. Its owner got out and came up the steps.

"Sorry to hear about the boy," Carmondy said as Ruben picked up the box of photographs. "Is he a relative?"

"His mother is my cousin," Ruben said.

"You think I could have one of those photos?" Carmondy said. "In case you need some publicity to help find him."

Ruben gave him one. "That's what Ms. Pray said. That we need publicity. That's why she's going to offer a ten-thousand-dollar reward for whoever finds Jimmy."

"That one," Carmondy said, watching Ruben drive off, "is like all families in these situations. Holding on to the belief that the kid is going to be found safe when we all know he's probably dead. Old Rosy's playing the odds. She always has courted publicity."

"Even so, maybe the reward will help. Keep people out looking for him," I said.

Carmondy wasn't listening. He was studying Jimmy's photograph.

"I tell you what," he said. "Have your sheriff put in a call to the L.A. police department and request a copy of the file on Dane Anthony. It was in nineteen sixty-three." Carmondy got to his feet. "He was arrested and charged with molesting a young boy. Later the parents refused to let the son be interviewed further, and the charges were dropped. Speculation was that the family had been paid off."

THIRTY

I sat for a long time after Carmondy's rental car made it out of the parking lot. Was I being used to help the man create a story where there was none, like Rosalinda Pray and the curse of Pancho Villa? There had to be such a file. There was nothing to be gained in making up something easily disproved. I thought of Jimmy. Of Dane Anthony inviting the child to come to lunch the day the insurance investigator had showed up. And all of us had been gone. Clay on a call, the crew and I at the village site, Nellie shopping in Presidio. Innocent coincidence or vile deliberation? I liked Dane. If all this came to nothing, I would be doing him a serious injustice. I went to telephone. I couldn't do otherwise, not with Jimmy at risk.

"I don't know how reliable his information is," I cautioned Dennis.

"Easy enough to check. Either there is a file or there isn't. I'll tell the sheriff. If the L.A. police can confirm this orally, we don't need to wait for the file to have a chat with Mr. Anthony."

I spent what was left of the morning in nervous apprehension, both about Jimmy and about how soon Dennis would arrive to have that "chat." Clay and I discussed it over lunch.

"You had to act on what Carmondy told you," Clay said.

"I know. Besides, I had the impression that Carmondy knew more then he shared."

"Probably he did," Clay said. "But he may have thought it best for the police to find out the rest for themselves. You did the right thing. It's up to them now."

Still, I worried. If Dane Anthony had been innocent all those years ago, I had provoked action that would cause him, at the least, embarrassment. I didn't want to think about any other scenario, because that would put Jimmy in even more jeopardy. Like Ruben, I wanted to believe in a happy ending.

Clay didn't have any afternoon calls, so he waited with me, but Dennis didn't show or call.

Scott, Jenna, and Chris came in for a visit after they finished taping at six. Scott said he had scheduled two early taping sessions for the next morning, one a retake because of a faulty cassette. He asked whether it was okay if they started at six-thirty. I told him that was fine. Chris showed Clay the script he'd been working on for the voice-over on the horse rescue video. He wanted Clay to check his commentary and left a copy with him.

After the crew left, we watched a movie on video, but without any enjoyment. We took our anxiety to bed with us.

THIRTY-ONE

I'd never spent as much time just sitting and waiting as I had since the video crew arrived. And thinking about the Trejo murder was easier than thinking about the present situation, so I made still another call at eight the next morning. I was going to have to take out a loan to pay the telephone bill.

Hap Boyer was at home. He asked after Clay, and I explained that he'd gone to Cinco's to do a progress check on some horses. Hap went on to the topic on everyone's mind.

"Bad about the Ramos kid," Hap said. "Me, I figured we'd find him hunkered down somewhere that first night. I still had hopes the next day. Now, this much time passing, it's looking bad."

I didn't tell him how bad it might be. My shift to the topic of the body he'd located forty years ago on No Man's Land started Hap on a detailed recounting, and it was some time before I got in a question about the contents of Trejo's pockets.

"Something that looked like an oversize locket? No, there

was nothing like that. The kids who found him were so upset at the sight of the body, their momma said they had nightmares. I doubt they'd have touched it, let alone gone through the pockets. The interesting thing about the case was that pickup of Trejo's. The Ojinaga cops found it on the streets. They said there was blood in the back. The sheriff said it proved Trejo had been murdered in Mexico. The cops said it proved nothing and kept the truck. Myself, I think he was killed somewhere else and the body dumped on the island. When Abelardo and me got to that island, there wasn't a footprint anywhere except the kids'. Me, I always thought whoever killed him might have driven out to the island, kept the vehicle in the water, and just pulled up to the edge of the island and shoved the body out."

And abandoned the pickup in Ojinaga, getting back by taxi maybe. I'd been driven all the way to the trading post on more than one occasion by an Ojinaga taxi driver. I was puzzling over the few concrete details I had about the murder when Dennis arrived. He stopped at the gas pumps. I went out to meet him, thinking the Carmondy story must have been a wash or he'd have gone straight to the RV for his chat with Dane Anthony.

I was wrong.

"Which one of those RVs is Anthony in?" he asked, slipping the gas nozzle into the tank. I told him.

At that moment, over Dennis's shoulder, I saw Nellie come jogging into the lot from his run and go into the RV. The gas tank had turned over six gallons when the door opened again and the nurse stood there motioning to us to come.

"Something's wrong," I told Dennis.

He turned and spotted Nellie, who gestured again. Dennis let go of the pump handle and ran for the RV.

I hung the nozzle back on the pump and followed him, arriving in time to hear Nellie say in his quiet voice, "It's Mr. Anthony. He's passed away." The nurse's T-shirt was dark with sweat, and perspiration dotted his forehead. Nellie stepped back from the door to let Dennis in. I was right behind him.

The actor was by the window in his wheelchair, his back to us, his head tilted slightly to one side, a book lying on the floor in front of him. The IV frame was to the right of his chair, the tubing running to his arm, as it had the morning I'd visited him. The bag looked nearly full of fluid to me.

Dennis walked around to stand in front of the dead man. I stayed put. Dennis bent over the body, touched a hand to Dane's neck, then straightened. He pointed at the IV. "What's this?"

"A liquid vitamin and mineral supplement. Mr. Anthony was convinced it did him good. His doctor said it wouldn't do any harm. This was the second treatment I've given him since we've been here. There's nothing in it that could kill him, if that's what you're thinking."

"What do you think happened?" Dennis asked Nellie.

"I don't know. When I left for my run, he was sitting there with a book on his lap. He read a lot."

"Let's step outside," Dennis said.

Dennis was last out. "What was the state of Anthony's health?" he asked the nurse.

"When I was hired, I was told that Mr. Anthony's only problem was post-polio syndrome." Nellie gave Dennis an explanation of that condition, saying, "He had massage therapy every morning. The only medications he took were over-the-counter analgesics for mild pain. He had a prescription for a muscle relaxant to be taken as needed. He hasn't taken any during the time I've been in his employ."

"How long is that?"

"I was hired for this trip," Nellie said. "He paid me extra for driving and cooking."

"Does this door lock?" Dennis said, jerking a thumb at the motor home.

"The key is in an ashtray on the coffee table." As Dennis turned to go back inside, Nellie said, "Would it be okay if I took some clothes out of my room?"

"I'll have to go with you," Dennis said, opening the door.

In less than two minutes they came out, Nellie carrying jeans and a fresh shirt.

"You're welcome to use the shower in the clinic," I said.

"Thanks," he said. "Deputy?"

"Go ahead," Dennis told him. "Wait, did he have family?"

"He wasn't married. That's all I know. His doctor is Louis Monroe in L.A."

Nellie went to shower, and Dennis locked up the motor home, then went to his car to call in the death. As he did so, Scott, Chris, and Jenna came out of the trading post and stood watching from the porch. I went to join them. Their shock, when I told them what had happened, seemed genuine but not deep, since the actor had been a stranger until the video project. I thought I saw a gleam in Scott's eye when Jenna mentioned the attendant publicity, making me think he had been around Rosalinda Pray too much.

We stood around the porch for a while and eventually ended up gathered around the kitchen table. All we could do was wait for the authorities to do their job. Nellie came in wearing his change of clothes, his hair damp from the shower.

Eventually Dennis came in and asked if everyone was there. Chris got up, saying he'd get Jeremy.

"He's probably sleeping," Jenna said. "Whatever he takes for his migraines really knocks him out."

While Chris was gone, Scott explained who Jeremy was and introduced himself and the others to the deputy.

Chris came back with Jeremy, who looked gray and drawn. He sat down at the table and shaded his eyes with one hand.

The deputy's first question was about next of kin. No one had an answer, and that was about as helpful as their answers to the rest of the questions Dennis asked.

By the time the sheriff arrived we were restless and bored with waiting and with one another.

Sheriff Skeeter Tate appeared in the doorway, looked around the room, then locked his eyes on mine. "I thought when the department went to the Sky Cell satellite radio units and people couldn't use a scanner to listen in to our calls, we wouldn't have crowds where we were trying to work. I'd have preferred you not make this death general knowledge."

"What are you talking about?" I said.

"I'm talking about all the people outside."

I got up and went to the front to look out the window. Polveños had begun to gather in respectful quiet in the parking lot, their faces turned toward the motor home where Dane Anthony lay dead, rosaries in their hands, their lips moving in prayer for the dead man's soul. Probably someone passing had seen the Sheriff's Department vehicle, spoken with Dennis, and spread the word.

"About this information you passed along to Bustamante." Tate spoke from right behind me. "You didn't take it on yourself to talk to the man, did you?"

I turned and faced him. "I did not."

"Did this writer fellow who told you talk to him?"

"No. I saw him get in his car and leave. Are you saying what Carmondy told me was true? I mean, Dennis did come to see Dane."

"There was a dropped charge all right. But no further complaints after that. Still, if Anthony had found out someone was digging up an old scandal, with his new television career, a family show and all . . ."

I thought of Dane's words about how good his life had been since the success of his show. "You're implying he committed suicide. If that's what happened, don't look to me. The only person I told was Dennis." I walked out, back to the others, and he followed. I had told Tate the truth, so why did I feel dirty? Dennis came in to tell the sheriff that the justice of the peace had arrived to officially declare the death. Tate flipped his notebook closed and accompanied his deputy out. We followed, grouping ourselves on the porch. In the RV lot the rear doors of a van stood open. Maria Gutierrez, justice of the peace from Presidio, came out of the motor home first. Then four men lifted the gurney bearing the bagged body through the motor home door and put it on the ground.

The crowd parted, many people crossing themselves as the gurney was rolled toward the open doors of the vehicle. Clay got back from Cinco's just as the actor's body was being driven out.

The sheriff made his way through the onlookers and back to the porch, put his foot on the bottom step, and looked up at us, saying, "I'll be in touch as soon as I hear anything." He walked away, passing Clay, who was rushing toward the steps, eyes locked on mine, saying, "What's happened now?"

The Polveños waited until the sheriff had left in his Crown Victoria, followed by the deputy's vehicle, before they, too, went home.

THIRTY-TWO

Mott, the newspaper reporter, called the next morning to interview me about Dane Anthony's death. I told him the little I knew because I owed him for giving me the information I had asked for, including Carmondy's telephone number.

"I guess this death will make that Pray woman happy," he said. "She can blame it on the ghost of Pancho Villa. I hear she's already calling the media, talking up that line and making herself available for interviews. Not for me, of course. Not now. I'm too small-fry."

I'd no sooner hung up than another call came in. I gave Carmondy the same details I'd given Mott. He sounded disappointed that I didn't have more to say.

"The sheriff claims he has no idea about the cause of death until he hears from the medical examiner. You were there with the deputy. Did he say anything to show which way he was thinking, murder or natural causes?"

"He asked about the IV," I said. "That's all, and you know the explanation about that."

"Yeah. Chelation therapy. Right up there with colonic enemas as a cure for what ails you."

"On the whole, I'd prefer the first."

"Did you do what I told you?" he said. "About the file?"

"Yes, but he died before they could act on the information. The sheriff wanted to know if I'd talked to him about it."

Carmondy gave a breathy laugh. "If he's thinking the old ham committed suicide out of remorse, he's wrong."

"You sound very sure."

"My bet, it's murder."

I felt cold. "Why do you think that?"

For moments all I heard was his wheezing. "I guess I can tell you. If it's not murder, it won't matter. If it is, all the old rumors about Anthony will surface and somebody will name names. I got my information from a retired L.A. cop. The kid Anthony was accused of molesting was Jeremy Win."

I sat down so hard I almost dropped the telephone. Carmondy was still talking.

". . . get an interview with him, maybe you could help."

I was silent for so long he took it for a no and tried a topic he must have thought I'd appreciate more.

"I haven't forgotten your interest in the Trejo murder," he said. "I've located the guy who was key grip on the movie. He played poker with Trejo quite a bit. He remembers him being angry and upset, and he swears it was with French. More important, he says Trejo and French had a private lunch in the director's trailer the day Trejo disappeared . . ."

I heard the words but I wasn't taking them in. I was thinking of Tom Putnam's words the previous morning, his reminiscence about a little boy sitting on Dane Anthony's lap.

THIRTY-THREE

If what I believed was true and Hugh had also been a victim of Dane Anthony's, my fear was that he was having an emotional breakdown. Why else cut himself off from everyone by dismissing the ranch hands and not answering the telephone?

A dust-eating drive of thirty miles brought me to the aluminum gate of the Wesleco ranch. Since the ranch was in high country, it got more rain and was cooler than our territory below. A mix of blue and black grama grasses grew on the outwash soils of the foothills. Time seemed to stand still in places like this, forty thousand acres of emptiness where mountain lions fed on pronghorn antelope and calves and black bears fed on the pads of the prickly pear cacti that clung to the pockets of soil in the limestone uplands, which eons ago had been the bed of a vast sea.

Once inside the gates it was another four miles to ranch headquarters. The main house rose to three stories in a series of stepped-back blocks constructed of cut stone that had been quarried in the upper canyons of the ranch. I was half blinded by the sunlight reflected against the large window of the top block overlooking the drive, but as I drove into the shadow cast by the house I thought I saw movement behind the glass.

I parked on the circular drive. Just as I stepped out of the pickup there was a loud burst of noise as the third-floor window shattered. I threw my arms over my head and fell back onto the pickup seat as a bronze sculpture of a bucking horse hit the cement a foot away and all around shards of glass landed with the sound of a hundred wind chimes.

"Hey, get me out," a half angry, half-tearful voice yelled. "He won't let me out."

I pushed myself up off the seat, slid out of the pickup, and stepped far enough back to get a clear view. Jimmy Ramos, rocking up and down on his feet and waving both hands, stood inside the third-floor room only inches from the gaping open space that had been the picture window.

"I see you, Jimmy," I called. "I'll be there in a minute. Stay back from the window."

I heard the click of the lock as I reached the door. I tried the knob. The noise had been someone locking the door rather than opening it. I knocked.

I tried to keep my voice calmer than my pounding heart. "Hugh? It's Texana. Please open the door and talk to me."

Behind the silence on the other side I sensed that he was there, standing as close to the door as I was.

I tried again. "Hugh, Jimmy's mother thinks he's lost somewhere, maybe hurt or dying. We have to let her know he's safe."

"He's not safe," Hugh shouted. "He'll never be safe as long as that man . . ." His voice broke, and I heard weeping.

"He is safe, Hugh. And so are you. Dane Anthony is dead."

Silence. Then, "You're lying."

"I'm telling you the truth. Call and ask anyone in Polvo. Better yet, call and ask Dennis and then tell him Jimmy is here with you."

More silence.

"Hugh, we have to tell Dennis that Jimmy is safe. It would be better if you did it yourself."

He opened the door and stood there staring at me. He'd dropped ten pounds since I last saw him. His unshaven face was as drawn and dry as beef jerky, and his eyes were so red they looked inflamed. "Is he truly dead?"

"Truly."

His eyes widened, then squeezed shut as he folded up. Simply crumpled over, arms hanging, hands on the ground, crying like a small child cries. I went to him, put my hand on his shoulder. He flinched. "Don't touch me. I can't stand to be touched."

"I'm sorry. Will you call Dennis?" His head drooped. I took it as a nod.

I stepped around him and went up the carpeted stairs. The observation room door was locked, but the key was on the table on the landing. I called to Jimmy as I turned the lock and opened the door. He came running.

"Mr. Wesleco locked me in up here," he cried.

"Are you okay?" I said, holding him. "Are you hurt?"

He shook his head.

"How did you get here, Jimmy?"

"I cut school. I was walking down to your place to hang, and Mr. Wesleco drove by and stopped. He asked me if I'd like to help him round up his cows. I wanna be a cowboy like him. He let me ride his horse. Then later, when I told him I had to get back to meet the school bus, he wouldn't let me. It was boring up here. No TV."

I took him into the den and let him watch television until Dennis, his mother, Ruben Reyes, Father Mario, and the nurse from the clinic in Presidio arrived an hour and fifty minutes later.

THIRTY-FOUR

Dennis let the boy go to his mother, putting them in one of the bedrooms with the nurse. Father Mario looked torn between the raw despair on Hugh's face and his duty to the child and his family, but when Sixta called to him, the priest went.

The rest of us remained in the living room that was filled with mementos of ranching life. None of us sat down.

"You hung up, Mr. Wesleco, before I could ask where you found the boy."

"Found? No, it wasn't like that. I was watching for him."

"Watching?" At that point Dennis cautioned Hugh and told him his rights.

To remain silent seemed the last thing Hugh wanted. He spit the words out as if they made him nauseous.

"I locked him in upstairs. It's very comfortable up there. There's a bathroom, and I put out blankets and a pillow for the couch. I fixed his meals and took them in to him. I never hurt the boy. I did it to keep him safe."

"Safe from what?" Dennis said quietly.

Hugh made a choking sound and looked down at the ground. "Him . . . *him,*" he wailed out the word. "Oh, Jesus, I can't even say his name." He rocked back on his heels and lifted his hands to cover his face. "He stayed in this house when I was ten. He came into my room at night. He touched me. Do you understand?"

I felt cold all over and hollow inside. "He's talking about Dane Anthony. He was the Wesleco's guest when *Panchito* was being filmed."

"Dane Anthony molested you?" Dennis said.

For a minute Hugh didn't respond except to tremble in a sort of spasm as he collapsed into an armchair by the fireplace.

Dennis went and got the nurse. When she came in, Ruben slipped out and went down the hall in the direction of the bedroom. The nurse took Hugh's pulse and felt his forehead. I could see beads of sweat dotting it from where I stood.

"When did you eat last?" she said. Hugh just looked at her. "Part shock, part hunger."

"I'll fix him something," I said.

"Something hot would be best," she added.

I rummaged in the kitchen cupboard and found only canned soup and cereal, and instant tea. The refrigerator was empty, but the freezer was stuffed with frozen dinners. Soup seemed the quickest. I picked cream of chicken. While it heated on the range, I boiled water and mixed the tea. A sugar bowl on the countertop had half a cup left. I sweetened the tea generously, poured it over a tall glass filled with ice cubes, put the soup into a bowl and set it on the table, then called to Dennis that the food was ready. He led Hugh in, holding his arm like you would a very old man's.

"Come over and eat as much of this as you can," I said, pulling out a chair at the table.

To my surprise, like an obedient child, he did as I said, eating mechanically, with little appetite, his eyes on the bowl. I sat down across from him.

Hugh managed about half the bowl. The meal did steady his shaking hands. He pushed the bowl away.

"For a long time after what happened I had nightmares. Then they stopped," Hugh said. "I began to think it was all just a bad dream. I forgot about it. Then that young man showed up about the video, wanting to know what I remembered about the moviemaking. After he left, I rented the movie from you and watched it. And remembered. He seduced me, I suppose you'd say. He was my friend. He made me feel special. Loved. Then, when it started, he said I shouldn't be afraid. That I would have to learn about such things, and it should be from someone who loved me. The things he did, the things he made me do, they hurt, but I still wanted the friendship, you see. Everyone liked him. My parents, the other kids, everyone."

From somewhere in the distance outside a cow bawled, a plaintive sound of need, a mother cow looking for her calf.

"You say you wanted to protect Jimmy," Dennis said. "Why did you think he needed protecting?"

Hugh didn't look at Dennis, but down at his hands, a flush of color on his drawn cheeks. "After I remembered, the nightmares started again. That's what Dane Anthony did for me. Kids outgrow their fear of the bogeyman. I haven't. I saw him that first day he arrived, holding Jimmy on his lap. That's how he started with me, holding me on his lap, reading to me. I knew he was after Jimmy, so I sat up on the hill above the trading post or in the trees across the river for days, watching him. Then someone spotted me. Those video people in a blue Range Rover."

"You were the man in the ghillie suit," Dennis said.

Hugh nodded. "I didn't want to be seen keeping an eye on the boy. I got rid of it after that and just drove around Polvo to be sure the boy got on the school bus every day. I had to stop him, you know who I mean, from hurting Jimmy."

"Did you try and stop Anthony another way, Mr. Wesleco?" Dennis said. "By setting fire to his RV?"

Hugh looked stunned. "I never did that." His eyes slid to

my face. "I wrote the warning note and pretended to find it on the porch because I was afraid of what I might do. When I heard about the explosion, that it was his RV, I prayed he was dead."

"And now your prayer has been answered," Dennis said. "If you'll stand up please, Mr. Wesleco. I'll have to take you in and get all this sorted out."

Hugh stood up. "You know the thing I can't get out of my mind now? He smiled and smiled, but he was a monster."

A shudder passed over me. "The devil always smiles," I said softly. I knew now why Jacinto Trejo had been murdered.

THIRTY-FIVE

Hugh, his face tear-streaked, ducked his head to get into the backseat behind the heavy wire barrier that separated the prisoner from the deputy up front. Ruben and the others had left minutes earlier. I gave Dennis a fifteen-minute head start before I followed. I didn't want to drive right behind Hugh as he was being taken to jail.

When Clay arrived home from doing a rabies clinic in Presidio, he found me looking at the movie poster for *Panchito* that Rosalinda Pray had given me. I had pinned it to the wall.

"That doesn't look bad there," he said, "but it needs a frame."

"It isn't staying up. I'm looking at what Jacinto Trejo saw."

"You've lost me."

"The horseman with the sombrero and the spurs. Not Dane Anthony as Pancho Villa, but Moxicuani. The devil who always smiles." I told him about Hugh and Dane and Jimmy.

"Poor Hugh. What happens now?"

"I guess he'll be charged."

Clay looked at the poster. "You think Trejo found out what Anthony was then?"

"Trejo tried to get Jon French, the movie's director, to stop what was going on. Tom Putnam heard him tell the director he'd given him enough time. I think Trejo confronted Dane himself, maybe in French's trailer that day on location. Some of the movie's crew saw Trejo go into the trailer. I think one of them killed him. Probably they got rid of the body together."

"No way to know now," Clay said. "With both Dane and French dead."

"There's something else," I said. "What if Dane *was* murdered? Dennis already suspects Hugh."

Clay considered it. "Let's hope it doesn't come to that."

"If it does, there's someone else to consider. Hugh said he didn't set fire to the RV. This morning Carmondy told me the name of the child Dane was accused of molesting all those years ago in California. It was Jeremy Win."

"Am I intruding?" Scott had come in from the front. "While you were out this morning, a man bought gas. Five gallons. He left a twenty." Scott handed me the bill. "He said he'd get his change later. I didn't get his name."

"No problem," I said. "How are things going?"

"We're moving ahead with the interviews. I think Dane would have understood the necessity of our finishing the project on time. It's a tribute, to him, really. Everyone has been very cooperative about all the rescheduling we've had to do. Jenna's upset, of course. She was very fond of Dane. She's superstitious, too." Scott looked a bit embarrassed as he said that. "Bad things come in threes, all that. First the explosion, then Dane dying suddenly. She's sure something else is going to happen."

I let him leave without telling him about Hugh. Would Jenna's count make that the third bad thing? It was to me. I hated what had happened to him, then and now. But the crew didn't know about that yet. Let them work in peace for a while.

The way news traveled, they would find out as soon as the next local came in to be taped.

It was long past lunch, nearly time for dinner. Clay offered to drive me into Presidio for a meal to take my mind off things, but I was too tired to face the drive. We had coffee with whiskey, which made me think of Rosalinda Pray and her Irish coffee. What would she do when she heard? I was sure she would find some way to capitalize on the publicity. After all, that was exactly what she wanted.

THIRTY-SIX

"What is she up to?" Clay said.

I crossed to the window to stand beside him and look out the window. Rosalinda Pray posed in front of the RV in which Dane had died as Jeremy Win took her photograph from various angles while Pippa the dog ran around in wide circles, barking.

I looked at the Seth Thomas wall clock. Even allowing that it ran ten minutes slow, eight-thirty was early for Rosalinda Pray to put in an appearance.

"I'll go offer her driver some coffee," I told Clay, "and we'll find out."

Ned Farmer sat in the blue Suburban out front, staring straight ahead as if in a trance. The set look on his face must have been boredom, judging by the speed with which he accepted my offer to come around to the back and have coffee.

"We were on the road so fast this morning, I didn't have time to do more than smell the bunkhouse brew," he told me.

"Ned, why don't I cook you some breakfast?"

Clay filled a cup with coffee for our guest while I heated a pan and cracked two eggs into a small bowl.

"How's it going?" Clay asked.

"Tell the truth, I'd rather be wrangling black bear than driving that lady."

"Temperamental?" I said, turning the eggs.

"You might say so. She's been in high gear the last few days since her 'dear friend' died. That's what she called that Mr. Anthony, but I tell you, she acts like his dying was the best thing ever happened—"

Ned stood up as Rosalinda Pray, carrying Pippa, marched in. "There you are, Ned. I'm ready to go now."

"I was just fixing Ned some breakfast, Rosy," I said. "Why don't you join us? How do you like your eggs?"

"I never eat breakfast," she said, freeing one hand from holding the dog to look at her watch. "I have to be back at the Alstons' by ten for a call from my publicist. She released an announcement about my reward offer for that missing boy."

"How much did you say this reward is?" Clay asked.

She raised her head proudly. "Ten thousand dollars for the child's safe return. The publicist said a nice round figure would look good in the headlines."

Clay's smile as he looked at me threatened to crack his jaw. "Texana, how're you going to spend that much money?"

Ned looked curiously from Clay, to me, to Rosalinda, who yelped, "What?"

"Jimmy Ramos is home with his family. My wife found him yesterday."

Rosalinda managed to not look too surprised, but the effort showed. "Wonderful. That's really . . . wonderful."

The eggs sizzled in the pan. Ned, who smiled almost as broadly as Clay, resumed his seat.

"Eat something, even if it's only toast," I said to Rosalinda.

Clay pulled out a chair for her. "Better do as she suggests. You'll want plenty of energy if you call a press conference to announce the boy is safe."

She shoved Pippa at Clay and sat down. The dog squirmed. I saw the spreading damp on Clay's jeans as the nervous animal emptied its bladder.

Gently, Clay put the little dog on the floor, then sat in the chair next to Rosalinda and said happily, "So, the ten thousand. Will that be cash or check?"

The actress choked down his kidding with the toast, asked for whiskey with her coffee, then left, saying she'd get back to me about the reward.

"You were a little hard on her," I said to Clay. "No wonder she bolted."

"That one wouldn't shy at a snake. Besides, she's never going to pay out on any reward."

"Not unless it would mean bad publicity," I said. "Where will you be today?"

"No calls so far. I'll be in the office."

After Clay went out, I telephoned the hospital in Alpine and talked with Gwen Masters. She told me she was scheduled to be released soon, but would be staying with friends in Alpine for two months of physical therapy.

"If I don't do the therapy, the doc says I'd be walking stiff-legged, like Chester on that old TV western," she said. "It's a good thing my neighbors are watching out for my cattle," she added. I could hear the wistful tone in her voice. Gwen was used to being on her own, in charge and beholden to no one. I said encouraging words about how fast the therapy would go and told her I would come for a visit soon.

"From what I read in the paper, you've got your hands full at home. I was real sorry about poor Dane, especially now that he'd got to be such a success with the TV show and all."

We talked for a few more minutes. I didn't tell Gwen about Hugh, trying to maintain his privacy for as long as I could. Any public revelation of what had happened would have to come from official sources.

For the rest of the morning, I did household chores while Scott and the crew worked steadily out front, people coming and going. Clay had a call at eleven and told me not to wait lunch for him. After Scott and Jenna and Chris took their noon break, I carried my sandwich and iced tea to the front porch. I was down to the crumbs and dregs when Hap Boyer drove up.

"I sure hope you're open for business," he said.

"The next taping isn't until one-thirty," I told him. "Come on in."

"Fence work," I said when he brought four pairs of work gloves, wire cutters, and a four-roll of baling wire to the counter.

"It never ends," he lamented. "You get one section repaired and you got to start on another." As I totaled the items, Hap added, "Heard about the boy being found. Good news that. Is it true what they're saying? That he was at Hugh's all this time?"

I confirmed that. Hap shook his head and asked no more questions.

"I'll be grateful when things around here get back to normal," he said. I think he meant Hugh as much as anything else.

I pushed the account book across for him to sign. "Say, I nearly forgot," he said, slapping the counter. "I hear Clay's got some new medicine for shipping fever. I got forty heifers coming in next week."

"Depending on their weight, one bottle will treat twenty-five to thirty head," I said, starting around the counter to get the medicine for him. "Two should do you."

"Stay put," Hap said, going down the aisle. "I've bought enough cow medicine here to know how to help myself."

"It's on the top shelf. Take one of the drug company's brochures, too," I called to him.

He came back with two large amber bottles and the brochure. I adjusted his bill, cautioned him to read the label and literature before using the new drug, and in case he didn't read the label, I emphasized that it was safe only for cattle.

"The stuff sounds more dangerous than a rattler," he said. "I'll be careful."

The video crew was coming back in as Hap left. I closed the register and got out of their way. Just as I got to the back, the telephone rang.

"I thought you'd want to know," Dennis Bustamante said. "We've released Mr. Wesleco."

I felt shaky with relief, but I didn't understand how it was possible for Hugh to have escaped charges.

"Jimmy's family refused to press charges and refused to let us talk to the boy. Ruben said Jimmy told them Hugh hadn't hurt him, and they're satisfied that's the truth."

"What does the sheriff think about that?"

"He questioned Mr. Wesleco a long time last night. After he met with Ruben this morning and talked with the nurse who examined Jimmy, he told the family about the old charges against Anthony in California and how they had to be dropped because the family wouldn't cooperate. I think that's what gave Ruben the idea."

So Skeeter Tate had depths to him I hadn't imagined, using the device that had allowed a guilty man to escape punishment to let an innocent man go free.

"The sheriff also cautioned Mr. Wesleco not to leave the county until we know the cause of Anthony's death," Dennis added.

"Any idea when we'll know what killed him?"

"We I-tenned the body," Dennis said. "It's up to the folks in San Antonio now."

"I-tenning" a body meant sending it straight down Interstate 10 to San Antonio. Presidio County was too poor to have its own hospital, let alone a medical examiner, so we farmed our autopsies out.

Did the deputy know that Jeremy Win had been Dane's earlier victim? Probably he did and was being discreet. If a retired cop would give the name to Carmondy, certainly someone among the L.A. police would tell the sheriff. Dennis hadn't asked me about Trejo's murder and whether I'd learned anything more about it. He had a present-day mystery to solve. Now as then, Trejo's death was a non-case.

I thought about how unlikely it was that I'd ever get any proof of my belief that Dane Anthony, with or without Jon French's help, had killed the *villista.* I took my frustration out on the garlic I was mincing for spaghetti sauce.

I was stirring the thickening sauce when Hap Boyer telephoned at four. "Say, I didn't notice till I got home and was reading that label, like you said. One of these medicine bottles has been used. Do I get a discount?"

"Used?"

"Yep," Hap said. "Rubber seal's got a needle hole dead center."

"How much of the medicine is gone?"

"Not much. There's just the one mark. The needle went in the one time, I'd say, unless the feller is a lot neater than me and hit the same spot every time. This stuff okay to use? You don't think it's contaminated or something? People do crazy things these days."

"Bring it back when you can. I'll give you another bottle."

I replaced the receiver and went to the connecting door. I could hear someone talking, so Scott was in the middle of a taping. I stirred the sauce and went back a couple of times to the door. As soon as it was clear, I slipped in. Scott was making notes. Chris was removing one cassette and putting in another. Jenna was just sitting. I went to the cabinet and checked the remaining bottles. The seals on all nine were intact.

The discrepancy didn't strike me until I was walking away. I went back and checked the shelf again. Nine bottles. There should have been only eight.

Maybe Clay had an extra he hadn't mentioned. A sample bottle the drug rep had given him. I'd ask when he got in. I went back to my spaghetti sauce.

Clay came in at seven. When I told him about the bottle Hap bought that had been used, he was upset.

"Maybe Hap made a mistake," I said.

"Not likely," Clay said firmly. "Hap's probably done about as much cow doctoring as I have."

"I also seem to have an extra bottle on the shelf."

"Extra bottle?" he said, frowning deeply. "Are you sure?"

"You got a dozen from the drug rep, right? You gave Cinco two, and I put the remaining ten on the shelf. Hap bought two, so that leaves eight."

He marched toward the front. I followed and watched him count the bottles for himself. He shook his head, his face puzzled. "Was I so tired that day we rescued the horses that I put the second bottle back into my case?"

"You rarely make mistakes like that," I said. "Come eat dinner. You'll feel better and think more clearly when you're fed and relaxed.

"No, I'll feel better when I've locked these bottles up."

THIRTY-SEVEN

Over the next four days Scott and his crew wrapped up the videotaping, starting early and working late as if they were as eager to be done with the project as I was for my life to return to normal.

Rather than delegate the duty to Dennis, the sheriff came himself to inform us of the medical examiner's finding.

Chris, Jeremy, and I were moving my shelving, tables, and stock back inside when Tate arrived, looking polished and impressive.

"We've got the autopsy results," he said. "Cause of death, undetermined. Manner of death, natural. Which means the medical examiner can't say exactly what caused Mr. Anthony's death except that it wasn't murder."

None of us cheered, but I think we all wanted to.

I walked the sheriff out to his car. "Cinco called Clay last night to say it looks like the horses and pony you helped us rescue are going to live," I said. "He thinks in seven or eight months he'll have at least three of them ready for adoption." I smiled. "He told Clay you had expressed an interest in the pony."

"Did he now?" Tate said, opening his eyes until he looked like innocence itself. He opened the car door, took off his Stetson, and tossed it onto the far side of the front seat, then slipped behind the wheel. I pushed the door closed. He rested his arm along the open window, looked up at me, and smiled, looking more relaxed and genuine than I had ever seen him.

"I figure any animal that survives being stuck under a collapsed roof for days must have a lot of heart. I'm retiring to a little stock farm in east Texas. I figure him and me can grow old together someplace with a little more rain and a little more grass."

Tate extended his hand out the window, and I shook it.

"Have you named him yet?" I asked.

Tate gave a big grin, turned the key, and started the motor. "I'm going to call him Bob," he said.

By eleven-thirty we had the trading post back in order. Scott and Chris were packing up their equipment. They would be leaving for Austin in the morning. Nellie would go with them, driving the RV in which Dane had died. Jenna had refused to move back into it, so she and Scott were doubled up with Chris still. From Austin, Nellie would catch a plane back to Los Angeles.

I spent a happy afternoon behind the counter, making sales and visiting with my neighbors who came in to hear the latest news.

That evening Scott grilled steaks outdoors for all of us, except Jenna, who added a skewer of vegetables for her meal. Nellie and Jeremy had set up folding chairs and a table, Clay had dug a pit for a fire to warm us and provide light, and he had iced the beer the way I like it, just short of frozen.

Dane Anthony was mentioned only once, and that obliquely by Nellie when he admitted relief at the medical examiner's finding. "I was sure Sheriff Tate thought I had poisoned the IV supplement."

Chris provided the after-dinner entertainment. He had edited the horse rescue video and finished the script, and he wanted us to watch it.

"Now that we know the horses are going to be okay, I don't think anyone will mind seeing the video." He looked at Jenna as he said this.

We settled into our living area, Scott and Jenna on the couch, Jeremy in one of the rockers, Nellie in the other. Clay and I each took an armchair. Chris put the cassette into the VCR and went to sit in one of the chairs at the table behind us.

"Wraparound sound," he joked, script in hand, ready to read. "Pretend I'm the pro with the really great voice who eventually will record this."

At his signal, I dimmed the lights and he used the remote to start the video. I was amazed at the quality of his work, the sharp, bitter images of the starved horses, the degree of shock he had caught on each of our faces as we viewed them, the undercurrent of emotion he had captured as we worked to treat each one, the intensity of our physical efforts to free the trapped pony. Then there was the contrast of the drive to Cinco's, the impact of the stark beauty and grandeur of the setting with the modesty of the house and buildings, the hustle with which the horses had been unloaded, fed, and watered, the concentration on the faces of Clay and Cinco as they talked. The last scene, which I remembered Chris had filmed while walking backward, showed their optimism at what had been accomplished.

At the end Jenna had tears in her eyes, and Nellie looked almost as emotional. Jeremy said quietly, "Brilliant."

Scott clapped a hand on his videographer's back. "That will be perfect when you edit Jeremy out of that last scene."

"I know," Chris said. "I was going to do that, but I thought it might make the scene too tight."

Clay and I looked at each other, clearly left out of all this technical and critical expertise.

"I didn't even notice him," Jenna said.

"I'll show you." Chris rewound briefly and stopped the tape,

Scott squatted beside the television screen, pointing with his little finger. In the background behind Clay and Cinco, Jeremy could be seen hurrying away from the barn, something in his hands.

"I had left my camera on the table and had to go back and get it," Jeremy said. "Sorry about that, Chris."

"No problem."

"That's not your camera, is it?" Scott said. "You can see it strapped over your shoulder."

"Must have been film I was holding," Jeremy said.

I turned the lights up. Scott went back to his seat. Chris started the rewind.

"The video is wonderful, Chris," I said. "I can't wait for Cinco to see it. Would you let me copy this tape to show him?"

"You can have this copy," Chris said. "I've got several. I'll mail the finished version with sound when I get it done." He looked at the others. "What do you guys think? Does it need music or not?"

"No music," Scott said. "The images should stand alone."

The rewind finished, Chris ejected the cassette and handed it to me as they said good-night and left.

I closed the door and looked at Clay. He read my face.

"You saw what was on the video, too?" he said.

I nodded. "You had to know what it was in order to recognize it, but yes, I saw. Jeremy came out of Cinco's barn carrying one of the big bottles of antibiotic. I was standing right beside him later that day when he took one last photograph of you with Cinco. By then, he must have had it hidden in those bulging pockets of his jacket."

"But why did he take it?" Clay said.

"It's lethal if used incorrectly, right?"

Clay went and poured us both a glass of whiskey. "In test animals, a single, small intravenous dose of that antibiotic killed in a matter of seconds." He handed me a glass and downed half of his in one swallow.

"How does the stuff work?"

"The mechanism of death? The antibiotic speeds up the

heart's rate and slows the contractions," Clay said. "In effect, the heart can't function. And it's all on the label. That's why it cautions users not to use an automatic pump syringe. Say a rancher hits his arm instead of the cow's hide. The pump syringe could force some of the antibiotic into a vein, and bingo, one dead rancher."

"Wouldn't it show up in autopsy as a heart attack?"

"It wouldn't show up as anything." Clay got up to replenish his drink. He added ice and poured the small glass full, then came back to the couch, sat, and looked hard at me, his face shifting into an expression so grim he looked like a stranger. "It wouldn't show as any type of heart damage, and it wouldn't show in routine toxicology screening. The animal toxicology studies were all negative."

"'Cause of death, undetermined, manner of death, natural,'" I said, quoting the sheriff. "Jeremy was standing right there when you explained to Cinco how deadly the antibiotic could be. And if Jeremy didn't understand that, all he had to do was read the label. We have him on videotape taking the bottle. Somebody used it. Somebody put an unaccounted-for bottle back on the shelves out front. Except now it's accounted for, and I'm afraid we know why."

"I wish I thought you were wrong," Clay said.

"I do, too, but it sure looks like Jeremy used the bottle he took to kill the man who molested him when he was a child. Then he hid the bottle in plain sight on the shelves with the rest of the antibiotic. A safe place, when you think about it."

"Most people wouldn't have noticed the single puncture mark the way Hap did," Clay said.

"And I'd never have counted the bottles and found the 'extra' one if Hap hadn't called me about the puncture.

"Jeremy told me he used to work in a hospital," I said sadly, "taking blood samples from patients, so he'd be comfortable with using a syringe."

"I'll tell you something else," Clay said. "The sheriff's report would have mentioned the chelation therapy, which means any needle marks in the arm wouldn't raise the medical examiner's eyebrows."

"Wouldn't Jeremy have injected the antibiotic into the IV."

"I wouldn't have," Clay said. "With his medical experience he'd know that the puncture might leak. And the forensic experts in San Antonio would have spotted a needle mark on either the IV bag or tube. Why risk raising the least suspicion when you're committing the perfect murder."

"Almost the perfect murder," I said.

We went to bed, not to sleep, but to talk in the darkness.

Clay would go to Chris as early as possible and see whether he and Scott had the equipment in the RV to enhance and enlarge the video image of Jeremy. I would call Dennis and tell him the situation. If we were wrong, Dennis had a long drive for nothing. If we were right . . .

The noise was like crackling paper, or—

"Fire!" I shouted, shoving back the covers. Clay was already up. We ran as far as the hall but the living area was draped in an orange sheet of flame. I felt the heat singe my hair and spun around, propelled by fear.

Clay grabbed my hand, shouted, "The window!" and pulled me along with him. He dropped my hand and raised the window, smashed his shoulder through the screen, lifted his legs over the sill, and used his body to clear the remaining screen out of the way as he tumbled to the outside. I was right behind him when he reached back to pull me clear.

A blast of heat and flame ripped his hands from my shoulders. I felt us fall together as wood and glass pelted us. I reached for Clay beside me. His pajama top was on fire. I rolled over him and smothered the flames with my body. The fire lit up the night. I saw blood on Clay's head and grabbed him under the arms and pulled, tugging him by increments away from the burning timbers. By the time I reached the edge of the parking lot, the trading post was engulfed.

"The bastard," I said, hugging Clay to me. "I should have known. He set fire to the motor home."

THIRTY-EIGHT

The dry timbers burned quickly as I sat supporting Clay's head and shoulders. Jenna crouched beside me, her arm around my shoulders. Chris and Scott aimed the water hose at the thirty-foot flames.

"They might as well pee on it," I said. Jenna giggled nervously.

The fire made so much noise we didn't hear the volunteers arrive from Polvo. Scott, silhouetted against the flames, pointed in our direction. Juan Risas came running to where we were clumped together on the hillside, stopped at my feet, and said, "I've sent someone back to Polvo to call an ambulance."

"Call Dennis, too," I said. "Tell him to stop Jeremy Win's Suburban if he can. It's red. Bright red. He left after he set the fire. Tell Dennis that Jeremy probably murdered Dane Anthony." And tried to murder us, I thought, looking down at my unconscious husband's face.

Beside me, Jenna started crying. She had been the one who

noticed Jeremy's vehicle racing out of the RV lot while Scott, Chris, and Nellie battled the flames.

The trading post had become a bonfire, and the volunteers had stopped dousing water on the collapsing walls and concentrated on keeping the flames away from the gasoline pumps.

Someone brought blankets, tucking one over Clay, wrapping another around my shoulders. The ambulance arrived an hour and ten minutes later. By then the trading post was embers.

The paramedics checked Clay over on the ground before lifting him to a stretcher. They asked me if I knew what had hit his head. I didn't. I walked to the ambulance and got in with him. During the three-hour ride to the hospital, one of the paramedics tended Clay, while another cleaned my face and hands of soot and put a light dressing on the burns I'd gotten smothering Clay's burning shirt.

In Alpine we were admitted through the hospital's emergency room. Clay was placed on a gurney, and a doctor came in to examine him while I lay on the next one over and a nurse with a clipboard came in to ask admission questions. Between questions and answers, I tried to hear what the doctor standing over Clay was saying to another nurse. Finally, two attendants came in and wheeled him out.

"He's going to X-ray," the clipboard lady told me.

I asked to stay with Clay, but they said it would be a while and they would let me know. Meanwhile, a nurse put me in a wheelchair and pushed me to a room. I removed my smoky scented pajamas, put on the hospital gown in the bathroom, and saw my face in the mirror. I looked sunburned. Heat-blast, the paramedic had said as he rubbed something on it in the ambulance. When the nurse came back, she had a glass of water with a straw and a pill in a paper cup.

"Take this. It'll help you sleep," she said.

I held out my hand, and she turned the cup over and spilled the pill into my palm. I put it in my mouth and sipped through the straw.

She turned the overhead light off as she left, but the light over the bed was on. I spit the sleeping pill out into my hand and sent it flying toward the trash basket. It missed, hit the wall, and bounced to the floor. I picked up the telephone, called the Presidio County Sheriff's Office, and left a detailed message.

I spent the first part of the night alternately worrying about Clay and thinking about Jeremy Win. When Scott and Chris had burst out of their RV thinking Clay and I were trapped inside the trading post, their first thought had been to fight the fire and try to get to us. Jenna, standing back, had seen me dragging Clay and yelled for help. Chris had run for Nellie, who did little but offer comfort and tell me to keep Clay still.

Bitterly, I thought of Jeremy. "He ran when he saw we got out alive," I muttered to myself. That was my last thought before sleeping, in spite of my intent to stay awake and pester the night nurse to find out for me how Clay was.

I woke sore and hungry and slightly disoriented. My father sat by my bed, dozing in the chair the way he had when I was in third grade and had measles, one of the rare occasions when I was sick.

When I sat up in bed, he blinked, then smiled. "Clay is okay. Concussion, the doctor said."

A nurse brought in a breakfast tray. "The doctor will be in to talk with you," she said kindly when I asked if I could see Clay. She adjusted the tray table in front of me and lifted the cover from the plate before scurrying out.

I looked at the watery eggs, pale toast, and foil container of jam and lost my appetite. I did pick up the cup of coffee and sip it.

My father reached inside his jacket pocket, brought out a sack with golden arches on it, and handed it to me. "I got this an hour ago. I doubt it's any colder than what's on the tray."

I dug in. Even the institutional coffee tasted better for the sausage and cheese sandwich. The wrapper was lying in the trash and the crumbs were cleaned off my mouth by the time the doctor arrived.

He was a young man in granny glasses, badly in need of a

haircut, and so thin I wondered if he ate the hospital food exclusively.

"No appetite?" he said, looking at the full tray.

"That stuff is better than a diet pill," I said.

He did the usual how-are-you-feeling-this-morning routine. I skipped straight to how Clay was doing. He said I could see him, but I mustn't be upset that he wasn't awake. I wasn't reassured by his explanation that Clay wasn't in a coma, that the brain was healing itself, and that he would wake up in due course. I kept my thoughts to myself, and as he left he promised to send a nurse with a wheelchair. Apparently, being ambulatory in the hospital was not encouraged.

After that, there was the little problem of getting dressed. The pajamas I'd arrived in were dirty and not for day wear. It was seven-thirty, two hours before the stores opened. And my father looked as if getting here and coping with the hospital personnel had vanquished his emotional reserves. I doubted he could cope with shopping.

We decided that I would put his jacket on over the hospital gown. I had arrived at the hospital barefooted, but the male nurse who came with the wheelchair also brought me a pair of disposable booties to wear.

My father accompanied me as far as the door but remained in the corridor as the nurse wheeled me to Clay's bedside. His face had been burned worse than mine and looked slightly puffy. Bandages covered his upper arms and chest. I spoke his name, but his eyes didn't open as I had hoped they would. I reached out for his hand and held it, as much for my own comfort as for his.

My father was gone when I came out. I knew he would be heading back to the ranch to recover his mental stamina after his foray into society. In his place, Jenna leaned against the wall. She gazed at the wheelchair I pushed ahead of me and said, "Aren't you supposed to be sitting in that?"

I stared at the grocery-size brown paper bag in her hand.

"Please tell me those are clothes, and please tell me they aren't your size." She was a foot shorter than me and weighed maybe 110.

She laughed outright. "I guessed your size. Ten, extra long. I brought pants and a shirt. And a dress, in case the pants don't fit. Also socks and tennis shoes and house shoes."

I took the sack, unrolled the top, and peered at something on top with blotches of red and blue.

"How did you manage to get anything at this time of morning?" I asked her.

"I called the owner of a local thrift shop at her home. She had her telephone number posted on the window. When I told her why I needed them, she came down and opened up."

"You're a lifesaver. Checkout time is nine. I hated to walk out wearing booties and a jacket."

We left the wheelchair by the door for the nurse to find when he returned and walked back to my room. While I dressed in the bathroom, Jenna talked.

"I drove the Range Rover, and Scott drove your pickup. We thought you'd need it to get around in. The windshield is cracked where the wall fell on it, but otherwise it seems okay. Scott booked you into the Best Western on his credit card. We thought you'd want to stay here in town with Clay."

I zipped up the pants. Better a loose fit than too tight. I buttoned the red and blue blouse, then squeezed my feet into tennis shoes that were a little short, but a better fit than the size twelve house shoes.

Jenna's tone had been drooping as she talked, so I stepped out to let her have a good laugh. "The colors do wonders for my face, don't you think?"

Her lips trembled into a smile, then she flew at me and gave me a hug, which hurt a little but was well intentioned. She stepped back, her eyes swimming with tears.

"We're so sorry this has happened to you and Clay. We never dreamed . . . I mean, Scott was so pleased when Jeremy called him and asked to work on the project and said his father had actually been in the movie. And he came highly recommended as a photographer."

"Jenna, I don't hold you or Scott in any way responsible. Just the opposite. You've been hurt by this, too." I checked the clock in the corridor. "It's eight-forty. Time to check out of here."

THIRTY-NINE

I stayed at the motel only long enough to shower. Then I drove back to the hospital and sat with Clay, sometimes talking to him, sometimes silent, but always watching for a hand movement or a flutter of an eyelid.

By three o'clock I was hungry enough to eat any number of hospital meals. Scott had paid for my room, but the motel had no dining room, and it was sixteen hours until the complimentary doughnuts-and-coffee breakfast in the lobby.

I debated calling my father, knowing he would come with some cash but also knowing the emotional cost to him of a second trip out among people.

Someone whispered my name. I turned around in my chair and saw a welcome sight. Dennis Bustamante. I joined him in the corridor. He asked about Clay, and I told him what the doctor had said. Then he gave me his news.

"We got Win. From your place, he took Pinto Canyon Road. The sheriff had already alerted the Border Patrol to help us search. Two agents picked him up before he'd gone five miles." Dennis grinned. "I have to hand it to Tate. When the dispatcher gave him your message, he acted on it. He locked Win up and let him sweat while he got hold of that videographer, Chris. The close-up of the tape clearly shows Win holding the bottle of antibiotic. By then Hap had brought in the bottle itself to check for Win's fingerprints, which we found, by the way. That Carmondy fellow had gotten in touch with the retired Los Angeles cop, who called Tate to confirm that Win was the child Anthony was charged with molesting. When Tate showed Win the copy of the case file, the videocassette, and the matching prints from the bottle of medicine, he broke. He started talking like the best thing that ever happened to him was confessing to murder."

Whether it was hunger or the emotional battering I'd taken since yesterday, I suddenly needed to sit down. "Let's go down the hall to the waiting area," I suggested.

"I have a better idea," Dennis said. He took my arm and led me to the cafeteria, then left me at a table. The large room was nearly empty, but four young female nurses at a nearby table gave the young deputy admiring glances as he walked through the serving line and came back with a tray loaded with two plates of food and coffee. "Ham or roast beef?" he said, setting the tray between us.

I took the closest plate and unwrapped the paper napkin from the cutlery.

Dennis said, "Win took a syringe from your supplies at the trading post to inject Anthony with the cattle antibiotic. He waited until he saw that Nellie guy leave for his run, then went to the RV, tied Anthony's arms with cloth so there wouldn't be marks, removed the IV needle, and injected him. After Anthony was dead, Win replaced the IV needle."

Hungry as I had been, my appetite vanished. I took no pleasure in being right about Jeremy Win murdering Dane Anthony.

"Win's first attempt at murder was setting the fire in Anthony's motor home," Dennis said.

"What about the trading post? Did he admit to setting that fire, too?" I asked, thinking of Clay.

"He did. He said when he saw your face as you watched the video, he knew that you realized he'd stolen the antibiotic. He was terrified that you'd put the rest together, especially after you asked for a copy of the tape. He took advantage of what he'd learned from the motor home fire, too. With the RV, the propane explosion surprised even him. With the trading post, it didn't take a fire marshal to determine arson. Win used the propane cylinder from Scott Regan's grill. Juan found the remains in the front room. If Win had put it in your living quarters, you and Clay would be dead."

"I don't understand what he thought he was accomplishing by trying to kill us," I said. "Chris had other copies of the tape."

"But only you and Clay understood what you were seeing on that tape and the implication of his taking that bottle of medicine. Guilt and fear can take a man a long way." Dennis drained the last of his coffee. "By the way, Win used gasoline from your pumps as a fire starter."

"I'll remember to put it on his bill," I said.

"The lawyers will have fun with this one," Dennis said. "A sympathetic jury may let Win off on the murder of Anthony. But trying to kill you and Clay, that was as cold-blooded as it comes in my book."

I thought of Hugh, of the emotional destruction he had suffered at the hands of Dane Anthony. "If Jeremy is cold-blooded, Dane Anthony made him so," I said.

We sat silent for a time. Dennis finished his roast beef, then said, "Clay will have to testify about the antibiotic."

"If he wakes."

"He will," Dennis said.

FORTY

Three weeks after bringing Clay home from the hospital, I sat hunched over plans for the new trading post spread on the table before me. We were living in the motor home in which Dane Anthony had died. Scott had told us to use it as long as we needed. Afterward he would sell it.

"You've got a letter from Rosalinda Pray," Clay said, letting the door bang shut behind him because his hands were full of catalogs that he dumped in a chair.

He walked around behind the counter and got a Coke out of the refrigerator, sat down on the couch and managed to contain his curiosity for five whole minutes before saying, "Well, are you going to open it?"

"In a sec," I said, extending a line on my rough plans in order to make the walk-in pantry larger. I would hand the changed plan over to the *adobero* from Ojinaga who was supervising the construction, already under way on the old site. I could look out the front window of the RV at the stack of adobe bricks brought over from Mexico and replenished weekly as the work progressed. Already the lower half of the walls were finished and the wide windows framed in. I would miss the old trading post but having a new home was exciting.

I tore open the envelope. A letter was folded around a check for ten thousand dollars. I waved it at Clay. "And you doubted my friend Rosy."

"I always believed she'd pay the reward," he said.

"I seem to recall a very different statement from you about that, mister," I said.

"What does she say?" he asked.

I unfolded the letter and read it aloud.

Dear Texana,

The publicity since the murder has been fabulous. That curse of Pancho Villa stuff worked great! Guess who's taking Dane's place on *Leo's Family*. Me! Me! Me! Jeremy's mother has hired some top-gun lawyer to defend him.

I bet you never thought you'd see this check. I didn't either, but my publicist said it would look bad if I didn't pay. I may not be much of an actress, but I'm nobody's fool when it comes to my own best interest.

You once asked me if there was anything odd during the last week of filming on *Panchito*. Dane's murder got me to thinking seriously about those days. There is one thing. I doubt if it's significant, but here goes. Jon French cut my lines in the final scene we were to shoot. So that morning I went to his trailer to ask why. I was so mad I didn't knock. I walked in and there was Dane standing across the table from Jon. He slammed this funny-looking piece of jewelry down on the table in front of Jon and and said, "There's the proof!" Then they saw me and Jon yelled at me to get out. Later he apologized and put my lines back into the scene.

Like I said, it's not much, but you asked. Funny, isn't it, if I'd known the movie was going to be such a flop, I wouldn't have given a rat's ass about a few lines in one scene.

Pippa sends kisses.

Your friend,

Rosy

"So you were right," Clay said. "Trejo confronted Anthony, and Anthony killed him."

"And Dane and Jon French were in cahoots."

Epilogue

Clay drove me across the bridge over the Rio Grande to Ojinaga and dropped me off at the bus station. I got out of the pickup with the straw carryall.

"See you this evening," I said.

Inside, I joined the chattering crowd standing at a counter, where tickets were sold through small holes cut in a chicken-wire screen, and waited my turn, all the while inhaling gasoline fumes strong enough to power a lawn mower.

Transportes Chihuahuenses operates eight buses a day to Chihuahua City. My destination, Cuchillo Parado, is midway between Ojinaga and Chihuahua.

The fare was cheap. I bought a bottle of water for the trip and boarded the bus, handing over my ticket to the driver, and found a seat near the back. Bus schedules in Mexico are fluid, arrival and departure times decided by the driver, who waits until his vehicle is full, according to his notion of what that word means. Our driver waited until standing passengers crammed the aisles. Finally, we rolled out of Ojinaga with *ranchero* music blaring from a tape player wedged on the dashboard, and for the next forty minutes we made reasonable time.

Cuchillo Parado is a town of forlorn, flat-roofed adobes, utilitarian and unlovely but comforting in its sincerity. The scattered homes were built crudely from the gray stone of the canyons beyond, with many still unfinished, though they have been standing for generations. Normally, it would have been a quiet place where sad-faced burros burdened with sacks of wood and straw stand in the street, dogs huddle in the narrow shade of walls, and people cluster in doorways to gossip. But on this day people crowded along both sides of the dusty main street and surged into the middle, forcing the bus to make a wide turn onto a narrow side street, where the driver parked and announced we would have to wait until the trail riders passed and that we might as well watch the parade. With that, he got out. I went with the rest of the passengers as we followed the driver to a crowded corner and watched the cavalcade of horses and riders go past the cheering crowd.

"What are we celebrating?" I asked the woman standing next to me.

"This is the anniversary of the first shots of the revolution. The riders are all descendants of the revolutionary fighters. They will end up in Ojinaga for the parade there."

We went back to the bus, and after much backing and turning and backing and turning, the bus driver got us back on the main street, drove five blocks, and stopped in front of a tiny whitewashed building, where everyone got off. The bus belched diesel fumes at us as it pulled away.

Inside the cafe, wooden shelves held canned goods and soft drinks in flavors like mango. Three mismatched tables waited for anyone who wished to order a meal from the kitchen, visible through an archway. I was the only passenger who'd come inside, which might have explained the look of perpetual disappointment on the face of the middle-aged woman behind the counter.

"*Buenas tarde,*" I greeted her. She rummaged up a smile. I bought a soft drink as a courtesy and asked if she could direct me to the cemetery.

"It is within walking distance," she said. "Go a few blocks more to the end of this street, and you will see it."

I thanked her and set out. In spite of the bright sun, the air was cold, but the walk warmed me. As she had said, at the end of the street, beyond the last house, spread over several sandy, grassless acres, was the *campo santos,* field of saints.

There was no gate or fence, and the graves, many very old, were not arranged in the rigid rows of American cemeteries but seemingly at random. Yet the place had a haphazard grandeur in the tumble of gravestones, the faded plastic flowers, the rosary beads dangling from crosses with plastic sheathed photos of the dead.

I crisscrossed the field looking for the marker and found it in a section marked with an old wrought-iron sign that had almost fallen over: The Cemetery of Dead Heroes. I opened my straw carryall and placed the wreath of red, green, and white paper flowers, the colors of Mexico's flag, on top of the grave of Jacinto Trejo.

Author's Note

In 1911, an American newspaperman visited a camp of the Division del Norte in Chihuahua. He noted the numbers of children, boys of ten and eleven, who were part of the revolutionary army.